The Radio Boys in the Thousand Islands

By

J. W. Duffield

The Radio Boys in the Thousand Islands

CHAPTER I

Vacation Plans

"Now, fellows, what are we goin' to do this vacation?" demanded Cub Perry as he leaned back in his upholstered reed rocker and hoisted his size 8 shoes onto the foot of his bedstead. "School's all over, we've all passed our exams, and now we've got a long vacation before us with nothing to do. It's up to yo-uns to map out a program."

"Why can't you help map it out?" asked Bud Taylor with something of a challenge in his voice. "You always have the last word?"

"Cub's the dictator of our outfit, and we do the work, that's why," declared Hal Stone. "We always have to listen to him, you know that, Bud. So what's the use o' kickin'?"

"Oh, I'm not kickin'," Bud replied. "It's no use. Cub 'u'd drown us out with his voice if we hollered. You know you made 'im admit once that noise was the only thing that 'u'd convince him."

"You c'n change that now and call it static instead of noise since we've all become radio experts," smirked Cub with characteristic superiority.

"Ha, ha," laughed Bud.

"Tee-hee," tittered Hal.

By the way, it was from this peculiar manner of laugh, that Hal got his nickname, Tee-hee. Cub's given name was Robert, shortened sometimes to Bob and Bud's was Roy. Cub and Bud were always known by their nicknames, but Hal was addressed as Tee-hee only on fitting or intermittent occasions.

The three boys were seated in Cub's room at the Perry home, one of the largest and most interesting samples of domestic architecture in the City of Oswego, on the shore of Lake Ontario. Cub was a rich man's son, but he was constitutionally, almost grotesquely, democratic. There was nothing that would make him angrier, to all appearance at least, than open reference in conversation to the wealth of his father. For such offense he was ever ready to "take off the head" of the offender. However, once in a while one of the bolder of his friends would beard the lion in his den more or less successfully. But it was necessary for such venturesome person to be ever in command of ready wit in order to emerge with a whole skin, figuratively speaking, and Bud and Tee-hee were the real leaders of this victorious few. That was the reason why they were chums of Cub.

The fact of the matter, to be perfectly frank, was that Cub was a good deal of an actor. Whether he was conscious of this fact we will not venture to say. He is the only one who knows, and we have never broached the subject to him. The average person on first making his acquaintance doubtless would set him down as a very domineering youth; some might even call him a bully, but they would change their minds eventually if the acquaintance continued. Perhaps the best way one could judge Cub, without being Cub himself, would be to characterize him as being fond of playing the bully just for fun. Indeed, it is quite probable that Cub carried a perpetual laugh in his sleeve.

This dominant youth was tall and lanky. He was only 17 years old, but as big as a man, so far as altitude and the size of his feet were concerned. He lacked one inch of being six feet tall, and he wore size 8 shoes. The hope for his proportion was expansion, and judging from the hereditary history of his paternal ancestry, there was good prospect for him in this regard. His father was a large man and well built.

To complete the description of Cub, he was a youth of very wise countenance. He liked to read "highbrow stuff" and reflect and inflict it on such victims as were unable to counter his domination.

Bud was a short, quick, snappy, bold fellow, "built on the ground". It is possible that he might have upset Cub in a surprise wrestle, but nobody ever dared to "mix" with Cub in such manner; the lanky fellow seemed to be able to out-countenance any suggestion of physical hostility. The glower of his face seemed to spell subjection for all the boy world about him.

But Bud would blurt out something now and then that seemed to startle Cub into a mood of reflection, and whenever Cub reflected his dominance wavered. Tee-hee was able to accomplish the same effect without a "blurt". Tee-hee was sly, "as sly as they make 'em", but it was a kind of slyness that commands respect. It even gave an air of respectability to his laugh, for, ordinarily, a "tee-hee" sounds silly. But Hal's "tee-hee" was constitutional with him, and his sly shrewdness gave it real dignity.

Cub was usually the dominating factor in all the boy arguments of their "bunch", which varied in numbers from ten to twenty, according to the motive of interest that drew them together. He seldom started an argument, unless his disposition to "bawl" somebody out for uttering a, to him, foolish opinion, he regarded as a starter. He seldom spoke first, but usually last. One day he "bawled" Tee-hee for the latter's "silly laugh", telling him that he would never be a man unless he learned to "laugh from his lungs".

"You seem to like a lot of noise," Hal observed.

"Yes, it's the only thing that convinces me," Cub shot back rashly.

He realized his rashness, but it was too late. Tee-hee "got" him.

"I understand you now," the sly youth announced. "Whenever we have a dispute, the only way for me to win is to make a bigger noise than you do."

But Cub was not slow, and he evened matters up by roaring:

"You can't do it; you ain't got the lungs."

However, there was a serious side to this trio of radio boys. They were not known chiefly for their frivolity, which probably would have characterized them if they had got into any bad scrapes. Their deportment was really above reproach, so that their parents reposed a good deal of confidence in them and allowed them to do pretty much as they wished in the matter of their recreation and sports. On the occasion with which the narrative opens we find them very serious minded over a very important problem, although it seemed well nigh impossible for them, even under such circumstances, to bar severely all manner of gaieties.

"I don't see where there's anything new for us to do this summer," said

Bud after the merriment over the "static repartee" with Cub had subsided.

"We c'n go camping or fishin', or we c'n stay at home and listen in."

"Oh, you haven't got any invention in that head o' yours, Bud," declared Cub with tone of disgust. "Tee-hee, take your turn and see if you can't hand us somethin'."

"Aw, why don't you furnish some brains for us, Cub," Bud objected with spirit. "I never knew you to yet. You just razz us till we turn up the thing all of us wants, and then you act as if you'd done all the work."

"Well, what do I pay you for?" Cub demanded, with an air of final judgment.

Of course, Cub did not pay them anything; that was just a little evidence of his exasperating domination. Bud saw, as usual, that there was no use of trying to carry his protest further, so he gave way to Hal, who looked as if eager to take his turn.

"I tell you what let's do," proposed the latter. "Let's go campin' and take one of our radio sets with us."

Cub leaped to his feet enthusiastically, bringing his feet down on the floor with a force that seemed to jar the whole house. Fortunately there was a substantial rug between his descending number 8's and the floor.

"That's what I call brains, Tee-hee," he declared, reaching over and planting a hearty slap on the author of this ingenuity. "You deserve a bonus. The scheme is hereby adopted."

"Without consulting me?" demanded Bud with very good simulation of hurt dignity.

"Absolutely, Bud, you fell asleep and let Tee-hee get ahead of you."

"And meanwhile, what did you do?" Bud inquired pointedly.

"I sat in judgment over your suggestions," Cub replied readily. "You fellows needed somebody to decide what your suggestions were worth. That's my function—get me?—my function."

"Well, I was goin' to vote for Tee-hee's idea," said Bud with slight tone of resentment. "You might 'ave let me get my vote in."

"It wasn't needed, it wasn't needed," Cub ruled. "Two's a majority of three."

"I'm going to vote for it anyway. I think his idea is a dandy."

"Your vote is accepted and recorded as surplus noise."

"Static, you mean," Bud suggested with modest sarcasm.

"To be up to date, yes."

"Tee-hee," laughed Tee-hee.

CHAPTER II

Tragedy or Joke?

The three boys discussed vacation plans along the line suggested by Hal for half an hour, and then Cub said:

"We can't get any further on this subject to-night. It's nearly 8 o'clock; Let's go in the radio room and listen to some opera music for a while."

He led the way into an adjoining apartment, a veritable radio laboratory. Two years before, as a wireless amateur, Cub had built for himself in this room an elaborate sending and receiving set, and he proved to be one of the first, boy though he was, to appreciate the outlook for the radiophone, even before "the craze" had gripped the country. He soon had his father almost as much interested in the subject as himself, so that the question of financing his latest radio ambition was no serious obstacle. An early result of this active interest on his part was the addition of a receiving amplification with which he could listen in to messages from major-power stations in the remotest parts of the country. Indeed, under favorable conditions, he had picked up messages from as far distant points as Edinburgh, Scotland, and Australia.

Cub sat down at the table and tuned to 360 meters. The other boys seated themselves comfortably and waited with a kind of luxurious contentment for the beginning of the program, which came in a few minutes. They "sat through" the entire Westinghouse program and then Cub began to "tune up and down" to find out what else was going on in the air. The room for several minutes was resonant with a succession of squeaks, squawks, whines, growls, dots-and-dashes, whistles, and musical notes. Suddenly he gave a start that aroused the curiosity of his friends and made them more attentive to his actions.

"Did you get that?" he shouted.

"No," replied Bud and Hal, in chorus, springing forward.

Cub was tuning excitedly back and forth about a certain, or uncertain, wave length, which he had lost.

"Put on your 'phones," he said, putting on his own. "You may not get it through the horn. I'm sure I got an SOS, very faint. I'm going to try to get it again."

Bud and Hal did as directed and listened with quite as much eagerness as that which was evident in Cub's manner. Several minutes elapsed before the search was rewarded. Then at last, in fairly distinct, although faint, vibrations came the distress signal again. All three heard it, and this time Cub caught the wave "on the knob" and did not let it go.

The operator sending the distress signal was evidently pleading desperately for attention, which nobody, it seemed, was willing to give to him. Several times he repeated his SOS, following each repetition with his own private call and wave length. Then he broadcast the following message in explanation of his appeal for help:

"I am marooned on island in Lake of Thousand Isles. I landed here from a motor boat with wireless outfit. Lake thieves stole my boat and left me here with outfit and little food. Will starve in few days if I don't get help. My call is V A X."

"Cracky!" exclaimed Bud excitedly. "Isn't that a thriller! He's an amateur and in trouble. We're in honor bound to help him."

"How?" demanded Cub derisively. "What can we do here nearly two hundred miles away from him?"

"We might get word to some police or lake patrol that'll go and take him off," Hal suggested.

"He's a Canadian," objected Cub. "Didn't you get his Canadian call? We'd have the time of our life getting a Government station to pay any attention to us hams. But listen, somebody's calling him."

All three listened-in eagerly, expectantly, wonderingly. Apparently this fellow also was a Canadian amateur, although he failed to identify himself.

"Oh, come off, you can't get by with that Robinson Crusoe stuff in this twentieth century," he "jeered" with all the pep he could put into his spark. "Some joke you're trying to play. What kind of publicity stunt is this, anyway?"

"No publicity," was "Crusoe's" reply. "I'll starve if I don't get help. You're doing your best to kill me. Keep out, I won't talk to you any more."

"I will not keep out," declared the other. "You're an imposter. I'm protecting the public."

"Whew!" ejaculated Cub, wiping his brow and snapping over the aerial switch. "I'm going to find out something about this."

A moment later his right hand was working the sending key with the speed and skill of an expert, while blue flames leaped over the gap with spiteful alphabetic spits. Hal and Bud watched him eagerly, and, with a skill indicating long and studied practice, read the message their lanky friend shot through the ether.

First he tuned for a few moments and then sent the call which had accompanied the first Canadian's "SOS". Then he threw back the switch and received a speedy answer. There seemed to be an almost spasmodic eagerness in the manner in which he sent his acknowledgment.

"I heard your call for help," was Cub's next cast. "Who was that fellow that snapped you up so sassy?"

"I don't know," answered the professed castaway. "I've been trying to get help for more than a day, and he always breaks in and queers my call. He makes everybody think I'm putting up a prank."

"Where is your island?" asked Cub.

"Somewhere in the Thousand Islands. That's the best I can locate it. I've never been here before. Where are you?"

"At Oswego, New York."

"What's your call?"

"A V L."

"Can you do anything for me?"

"I don't know what I can do unless I try to interest somebody near you by wireless. I'll send out a broadcast in any manner you may suggest. But you can do that just as well as I."

"I have done it over and over, but it does not do any good," said "Crusoe". "That evil genius of mine always manages to queer me. Finally I got so desperate that I sent out an SOS."

"And committed a radio crime," broke in the alleged evil genius. "Don't you know the rules governing that distress signal?"

"There he is again," "Crusoe" dot-and-dashed.

"Who are you?" demanded Cub.

"I am Canadian amateur," was the reply. "That fellow who sent the distress signal is a Canadian college student trying to put over a college prank. I am on his trail to prevent him. We have a wager up; if he induces anybody to go to his rescue, I lose."

"That is not true," interposed the sender of the SOS.

"What is your call?" Cub inquired.

"Yes, give it to him, and tell him what college I am from," proposed the "fellow on the island".

"One of the conditions of our wager is that I must not reveal my identity," returned the anonymous amateur. "He's bound by like terms. He does not dare give you his name and address."

"That fellow is insane or a villain," declared "Crusoe". "I do not know who he is, but if I starve to death, he'll be a wanton murderer. My name is

Raymond Flood. I am not a college student. I am a high school student at Kingston."

"Is his name Raymond Flood?" was Cub's next query intended for the anonymous amateur.

"No," was the latter's reply.

"What is it?"

"Under terms of our wager, I must not reveal his name and he must not reveal mine."

"Whew!" exclaimed Cub, addressing his two friends, who removed the phones from their ears, the better to hear him. "Can you beat that?"

"We sure have hit a sensation of some sort," Hal declared.

"What'll we do?"

"I don't know what under the sun to do," Cub replied. "I don't like to pass him up, for fear he may be telling the truth; and yet, I don't like to be the victim of a joke."

"I tell you what to do," Bud suggested, without any seriousness of intent, however. "Make a dash over the lake in your father's motor boat and rescue this Robinson Crusoe."

"By Jiminie, Bud!" exclaimed Cub enthusiastically! "You've hit the nail on the head. Our vacation problem is solved. That's what we'll do, all of us. I don't care whether it's a joke or a tragedy; we'll make a voyage of discovery over that way and see if we can't find Crusoe's island. What say you, fellows?"

CHAPTER III

Talking It Over

What could the fellows say?

They couldn't say anything at first, so astonished were they at the announcement from Cub. Then so great was their eagerness, following the recovery from their astonishment that about all they could do was to "fall over each other" in their efforts to express their approval.

At last, however, the "panic of joy" subsided, and they began to sift out the obstacles that must naturally obtrude themselves in the way of such a scheme that involved such departure from the ordinary course of events.

"Do you think your father will let us go?" asked Hal somewhat apprehensively.

"We've taken trips alone before," Cub reminded.

"Yes, but only for short trips along the shore or up the canal," Hal replied. "Ontario's a rough lake, you know."

"Yes, but safe enough if you're used to it," Bud reasoned, coming to the aid of his lanky friend. "If necessary, we could follow the bend of the shore all the way and never get out of sight of land."

"That would make the trip longer and consequently take so much more time to get there," reasoned Cub.

"Time's precious in a case like this," Hal averred. "Remember that we must get up there in time to save a fellow with no food on hand from getting an empty stomach."

"How long would the trip take?" asked Bud.

"Well, let's see," said Cub, picking up a pencil and beginning to figure on a tab of paper before him. "The Catwhisker can make twelve miles an hour under favorable conditions. We could start early in the morning and reach the Thousand Islands surely by noon, and then have the rest of the day to hunt for Mr. Robinson Crusoe."

"It might be like hunting for a needle in a haystack," suggested Hal dubiously.

"Why shouldn't we be able to find him?" Cub demanded.

"It depends on how well Mr. Crusoe can describe his surroundings for us and how well we can follow directions," Hal argued.

"That's true enough," Cub admitted. "Let's see if I can get 'im again and what he can tell us."

He had no difficulty in picking up the "desperate Mr. Crusoe" again, for the latter proved to be "sparking" the ether with frantic calls in search of the radio boy on whom he believed he had made a serious impression, but who seemed, for some unhappy reason, to have forgotten him.

"I was just discussing your case with a couple of friends," Cub explained. "We thought we might make a run down your way in a motor boat if you could give us a clear idea where your island is located."

"I can't give you any latitude and longitude," was the "islander's" reply. "I was captured in my motor boat only a mile or two away from home. Then I was blindfolded and put here on this island by the rascals. It's a small wooded island surrounded by several other small wooded islands, making it impossible for me to hail passing boats. I will be glad to pay your expenses and enough more to make it worth your while if you will find me and get me away from here."

"I don't know how we'd find you without cruising among the Thousand Islands a week or two," returned Cub. "Have you a flag of distress flying?"

"It wouldn't do any good. Nobody would see it."

"Oh, I have an idea!" suddenly exclaimed Hal, for he and Bud had put their receivers back on their ears when Cub began to communicate with "Mr. Crusoe" once more.

"Hold the wireless while I talk with my friends," Cub directed to the fellow "at the other end of the ether". Then he removed the phones from his ears, and the other boys did likewise.

"Well, what's your idea, Tee-hee?" the operator demanded with something of a tone of business challenge.

"Why, all we need is a radio compass," Hal replied. "You know I made one last summer, although I didn't have much use for it. We can install it on the boat and make a bee line for that fellow's island if he keeps his spark busy to guide us."

"Good!" exclaimed Bud. "That'll settle the biggest problem before us."

"Yes," Cub agreed. "You're a regular Thomas Edison, Jr., Tee-hee. I think we'll have to elect you captain of this expedition."

"If we make it," Bud conditioned with a slightly skeptical grin.

"My opinion, if it's worth anything to you guys," said Cub; "is that we'd better map out our plan thoroughly before we say anything about it to our fathers. Then we can put our arguments in convincing manner."

"We must finish our plan to-night, for we ought to start not later than Wednesday morning," Bud argued. "That'll give us one day to get ready in."

"We'll need all that," said Hal. "Now, let's get busy, boys, and see how near our plan is finished. It's after 10 o'clock, and I'll have to go pretty soon. If we go, we'll need—"

"Some food," itemized Bud.

"Yes, enough for us and to feed a starving Robinson Crusoe," amended Cub, beginning the list on a fresh sheet of paper.

"And drinking water."

"No. 2," commented Cub, as he jotted it down.

"And we ought to have a wireless set on hand," Hal suggested.

"Sure," said Cub. "You bring that and your loop aerial. This set is too big to transfer on board very well."

"That about completes the list, doesn't it?" asked Bud.

"We'll have to have a permit," said Hal.

"Permit for what?" Bud inquired.

"A permit from Mr. Perry to go."

"You're kidding now," said Bud. "Maybe you think this is all a joke."

"I'm afraid it is, but I'll eat my words—and glad to do it—if Cub's father and our fathers let us go."

"We've all got some persuading to do, there's no doubt o' that," Cub admitted; "but I hope we'll succeed. I'll talk to father in the morning at the breakfast table and call you fellows up an' let you know what he says. Now I'll call Mr. Robinson Crusoe again and tell 'im I'll call 'im in the morning and let 'im know what we can do."

He had no difficulty in getting the "island prisoner" again, for the latter was waiting eagerly for a message of hope. Cub, however, was cautious in this regard, saying nothing about the plan of himself and his two radio friends. He merely told "Mr. Crusoe" that he would do the best he could for him and would call him next day, specifying the hour. Then Bud and Hal went their separate ways homeward.

At 8:30 next morning Cub called Hal on the telephone and inquired:

"Hello, Hal, did you talk to your folks about our plan?"

"Yes," was the reply; "and I just got through talking with Bud over the wire before you called up."

"Well, how does it stand?"

"His folks won't let him go and my folks won't let me go unless some experienced man goes along with us."

"Hooray! we win!" yelled Cub. "Father thinks it's a peach of an adventure and he's almost as crazy over it as we were last night. He says 'yes' with a capital Y, and he'll go along with us. He says he's been wanting a vacation with some pep in it for quite a while, and this scheme of ours is ninety-nine per cent pep. If you and Bud don't go, father and I are going anyway. So get busy as fast as you can. We're off this afternoon, as early as we can get ready. I've already sent a wireless to Crusoe that we're coming. Good-bye; I'm going to call Bud now. Be over here as soon as you can and help us get ready."

CHAPTER IV

The Catwhisker

The Catwhisker, a neat gasoline power boat of the cruiser type left the private dock of the Perry home in Oswego early in the afternoon with the three radio boys and Mr. Perry on board. This had meant some rapid work by the members of the "rescue party" in preparation for the trip, for it was necessary for them to do considerable buying in the line of provisions and the transportation of a number of articles of incidental convenience, together with one complete sending and receiving wireless outfit. The hook-up of this outfit, on the boat, however, was left for a more leisurely occupation after all other preparations for the cruise were completed and they were well on their way.

The name Catwhisker harked back to the days when radio, or wireless telegraphy, was in its infancy in the experience of the three boys whose adventures are the inspiration of this volume. Mr. Perry bought the motor boat at a time when his son and the latter's two chums were busy experimenting with crystal outfits, and the name of the cruiser was suggested to them by the fine spring-wires used to make contact with the crystals in their detectors. No doubt, it was the catchiness of the word, as well as its association with their hobby, that appealed to them in the general search for a name for the boat.

This vessel was 36 feet long, with a beam of nine feet and with a canopy covering the after deck. Amidships was a raised bridge deck on which were mounted and housed the wheel and engine controls. Under this and the after deck were the engine-room and the galley, and forward of these were the cabin and two small staterooms. At the bow and in the stern were two tall slim masts that had been erected solely for the extension of a radio aerial. The hull was painted white with a blue stripe midway between the bridge-deck level and the water line.

Cub and his father were real chums in matters of boating. Mr. Perry, although ordinarily a man of very neat appearance, on the present occasion had discarded his usual sartorial excellence and appeared on the Catwhisker in clothes easily associated with cotton waste and oil cans. Indeed, he could take care of the engine quite as well as his son, who was an amateur expert, and seemed to enjoy discharging his full share, of all the "overall and apron tasks" on board.

Mr. Perry took charge of the wheel and engine controls of the yacht at the beginning of the cruise, so that his son and the other two boys were left free to perfect the hook-up of the radio set supplied by Hal. First, two wires, attached to spreaders at both ends, were extended between the two masts for an aerial, and a lead-in was arranged through one of the windows of the cabin. On a fixed table near this window they anchored firmly the various portions of Hal's sending and receiving set, in order that these might not be thrown down and damaged if the lake should become rough. As the apparatus was supplied with two steps of amplification, Hal had brought also a loud-tone horn to facilitate occasional parlor entertainment should they have leisure to listen-in to programs from various broadcasting stations within their receiving range in the course of their cruise.

Hal's outfit was by no means as elaborate or as expensive as was Cub's, but it was sufficient to receive radiophone programs, under favorable conditions, from the strongest stations 300 or 400 miles distant, while the strong spark of his code transmitter had earned for him a wide acquaintance in amateur circles.

Before they started, Cub had another dot-and-dash tete-a-tete with "Mr. Crusoe", acquainting the latter with the latest developments of their plan and requesting him to call the Catwhisker regularly at half-hour intervals if the more limited set they would take with them proved insufficient to reach him from the start.

"When we reach the Thousand Islands, we will get busy with our loop aerial and find you by radio compass," he promised.

The mysterious intermeddler who professed to have a sporting wager with the "island prisoner," was on hand with a machine-gun stream derisive waves, but Cub refused to pay any attention to him, not that he regarded that fellow's version of the affair as utterly unworthy of consideration, but, for the time being, at least, he did not wish to believe it. He was eager for the adventure, which might be spoiled if his father became convinced that "Mr. Crusoe's" SOS was a gambling hoax.

The boys took regular turns at the radio table in the cabin that afternoon and found the occupation of listening-in much more interesting than it had been at their homes, not because of any particular difference in the messages, but because of the more romantic character of their new motives and surroundings. Even the multitude of static interferences that swarmed the atmosphere on this, the first oppressively hot day of the season, were combatted with tuning coil, condenser, and detector, so confidently, although with poor success, that Mr. Perry pronounced them all "princes of patience".

In other words, the boys were in the best of spirits, all handicaps notwithstanding. Cub's father had not taken his first lesson in wireless telegraphy, and so left the radio field entirely to the three young amateur experts. In spite of the heat, they were able to get a more or less broken message now and then from the "island prisoner", but could get no acknowledgment of receipt of messages sent by them until about supper time.

"If it weren't for this heat, we probably could 'ave got a message to him as we were leaving Oswego," Cub remarked to Bud after they had been on the lake about two hours.

"The atmosphere is the worst I've ever known it to be," returned Bud, who had been laboring hard with key and spark for some time. "If it don't clear up, we may not be able to begin our hunt for him before morning."

"Well, we'll go along until half an hour before dark, I suppose, and then find a place to tie up till morning," said Cub.

He consulted his father on the subject, and the latter indorsed the plan.

The lake was rather choppy, in spite of the calmness of the day; consequently, the Catwhisker was unable to make a record run to the head of the St. Lawrence River. Ontario is not a placid lake, although it has not the heavy roughness that characterizes Lake Huron. A strong current is driven through its middle by the flood of the upper lakes after its plunge over Niagara Falls, and along the shores is a back-sweep of eddies and swirls. Hence the pilots and shippers of small boats on the lake, if they are wise, keep their weather eyes well peeled for any disturbance that may augment the natural roughness of this body of water.

Mr. Perry and his three boy companions were all well aware of the wisdom of weather caution while cruising in the Catwhisker. In the morning before starting, they had consulted the Government forecast and found the outlook favorable, but they were well aware of the fact that absolute dependence should not be put upon even so learned a being as a Great Lakes weather man.

Bud made the first score in the frequent attempts to get a message to the "island prisoner". Conditions in the ether became much better toward evening when a cool wind began to blow. Just before sending the message that reached its goal, Bud received the following from VAX:

"Where are you? Can't you reach me? Nobody in sight yet. Ate my last crust of bread an hour ago. Have to drink lake water to keep alive. Try again to get a message to me."

Bud tried again and received the following reply:

"Got you faintly. Try again. Where are you?"

But fifteen minutes elapsed before the boy at the key was able to score again. After that, however, they had no difficulty in reaching "Crusoe island" with key and spark.

Then arose the question as to whether they should attempt to find the "radio Crusoe's" island that evening or should seek a suitable mooring place and postpone the search until morning.

"There's one matter to be taken up before we decide to go much further to-night," said Mr. Perry, who had just turned the wheel over to Hal and joined the conference in the cabin.

"What's that?" asked Cub.

"The weather. We're right at the beginning of the Thousand Isles now, but we can have a nasty time of it anywhere in the upper part of the river in a storm. The wind is getting pretty lively, and you know how much the temperature has dropped."

"Oh, I can take care of that," Bud declared eagerly. "I've been having a chat with a 'ham' somewhere along the coast. I'm sure he'll get the evening forecast for me."

As he spoke, Bud dropped his eye on the log where he had made note of the shore "ham's" call and then began to tune for his wave length. To his gratification, he found the fellow busy with his spark and waited till the message was finished; then he threw his aerial switch into sending and lettered the call. The "ham" answered and asked what was wanted.

"I want the weather forecast for to-night," Bud replied. "We're out in a motor boat and want to know if it's safe to stay out till dark."

"I'll get the latest by telephone and call you back in a few minutes," was the operator's generous offer.

Ten minutes later the promised call came, thus:

"Clear to-night. Wind brisk, but not violent."

Cub was listening-in and read this message to his father.

"That means we can go on nearly three hours yet before we have to seek a post for the night," the latter announced.

"Good!" exclaimed Cub. "Now I'm going to test that radio compass and see what may be expected of it in the morning if we don't find Mr. Crusoe to-night, which isn't very likely."

Preparation for the test was simple and quickly made. The loop aerial, a collapsible affair, was set up in the cabin and connected in such manner that it could be used for receiving simultaneously with the use of the outside aerial for sending.

While Cub was thus occupied, Mr. Perry set a hasty supper of prepared foods on the table and "ate a bite". Then he returned to the chart and wheel house and relieved Hal, sending the latter back to the cabin for his meal and for further radio consultation with the other boys.

CHAPTER V

A Baffling Situation

The compass worked admirably. Although the principle of the affair was very simple, Hal must be given credit for having done his work well.

So satisfactory did the device prove from the moment when it began to take messages from the "island prisoner", that all on board the Catwhisker became hopeful of success before sun-down. "V A X" kept a stream of waves leaping from his aerial for their guidance and the motor boat chug-chugged along like a hunting hound made more and more eager by the increasing excitement of the hunt.

"I wonder what's become of the fellow who tried to head us off," remarked Hal as he left the supper table and prepared to relieve Cub at the wireless. "You haven't heard anything from him, have you?"

"No, not a thing all day," Cub replied. "I guess we've tired him out. Did you get anything from him, Bud?"

"Not a shiver of the wires," answered the latter.

"Maybe he's given us up as hopeless easy marks," Cub suggested.

"Why, do you think his story is true and 'Bobby Crusoe' is a fake?" asked Hal.

"I don't know. I wouldn't be surprised to find almost anything—or nothing—as we get near to the end of our hunt."

"But he must be on the island," Bud reasoned. "And he must have a wireless set, or he couldn't have sent the messages we got. That much is certain."

"Not all of it," Hal objected.

"Why?" Bud demanded.

"Maybe he isn't on an island."

"You mean, maybe the whole thing's a fake—eh?"

"Maybe."

"If the whole thing's a fake, then that other fellow who tried to head us off must 'ave been a party to the game," Cub interposed.

"There wouldn't be much sense in that," said Bud.

"I agree with you," Cub continued. "The scrap between those two hams was genuine enough."

"But they were holding something back from us," Hal declared.

"Both of them?" asked Bud.

"I shouldn't be surprised."

"Nor I, either," said Cub.

"Then they've put one over on us," was Bud's inference. "Are you sorry we came?"

"I? No, sir!" Cub emphasized. "It's a dandy adventure, whatever the result. I didn't swallow that Crusoe story whole at any time."

"Neither did I," said Hal.

"I thought there were some funny things about it," Bud announced reflectively; "but I didn't know how to put them together or take 'em apart."

"That was my fix," said Cub; "and it's my fix yet."

"I guess we all agree that the whole affair is very strange," Hal concluded. "We really don't believe we've been told the truth, and yet we get in worse trouble when we try to make something else out of it."

"I wonder what your father thinks about it, Cub," said Bud.

"Oh, he accepts it at its face value for the sake of the adventure," the tall youth replied. "But he's wise enough to know there may be a lot of hocus-pocus in the business."

For nearly two hours the motor boat wound its way at a fairly good clip among the picturesque islands of the upper St. Lawrence, the radio compass fixing the course as certainly as the hunter's pursuit is directed by the nose of his hound. They had no way of telling, at any time, how far ahead was the object of their search, but they had the satisfaction of knowing that they were constantly approaching it. At last an unexpected climax threw their hitherto clear prospect into confusion. This climax grew out of a series of confounding messages from the "lost islander".

"I see you coming," was the first of these messages.

"Where is he?" asked Cub and Bud in chorus. Hal was at the table and the other two boys were listening-in.

"I don't know," replied the operator. "One of you boys go on deck and see what you can see."

Cub dashed up the companionway two steps at a time. In a few moments he returned with the announcement:

"There's an open stretch of four hundred yards ahead of us. He's probably on the island at the other end. I'm going back on deck and watch for developments."

There was a speaking tube communicating between the pilot house and the cabin and through this Cub kept his boy friends acquainted with the progress of the search. They reached the island in question, but not a sign of human life was discoverable on it. The motor boat passed around it, and meanwhile the radio-compass found the strength of its receiving directly down stream. Cub communicated this condition to the cabin, and Hal dot-and-dashed the following to "VAX":

"Where are you? We can't see you."

"I saw you," was the reply. "I climbed a tree and saw you headed right for this group of islands."

"No, no," objected Hal. "It must be another yacht."

"Aren't you a white cruiser with awning mid and aft, and pilot house on bridge deck?" asked "VAX".

"Yes," answered Hal.

"There's somebody calling us," remarked Bud at this point.

"Yes, I get 'im," returned Hal. "Why, it's the mysterious guy who tried to head us off night before last and yesterday."

Both boys read the "mysterious guy's" first send with eager impatience.

It was as follows:

"He's making sport of you. Mark my word, when you reach the island, he'll be gone."

"Keep out, you pirate," ordered Hal.

"All right, but you'll call yourselves a bunch of fools."

The next instant the "island prisoner" broke in thus:

"Hurry; they are after me. I think they are the ones who marooned me here. Their boat looks like yours, I guess."

"See!" exclaimed Bud. "This makes things look bad. If those fellows are robbers they're armed. We haven't a gun on board, and if we had we wouldn't want to get in a fight over an affair that looks more like a joke than a tragedy."

"And yet it may be a tragedy," said Hal.

At this moment Cub reappeared in the cabin and the situation was explained to him.

"It begins to look like a tragedy," he admitted; "and yet if we treat it as a tragedy and it proves to be a joke, we'll feel like a comedy of errors."

"Now, you're getting highbrow, Cub," was Hal's mock objection.

"It's common sense, isn't it?" the youthful philosopher reasoned.

"Yes, but you forget one thing," the sly-eyed Hal rejoined: "With so much

Q R M, it's very hard to pick out common sense in an affair like this."

"That's true," replied the other. "We've had more interference in this trip thus far than anything else."

"And the big question now is, how're we goin' to tune it out?"

"I confess, I'm stumped," said Cub. "Guess we'll have to refer the whole matter to father, but I bet he'll be up against it just as much as we are."

Cub turned toward the companionway with the intention of seeking an interview with Mr. Perry in the wheel house, but Hal delayed him again.

"Wait a minute," said the operator. "Here's our island friend again."

Cub and Bud donned their phones once more. The message received was more startling than any preceding.

"They are coming ashore," was dot-and-dashed into the three boys' ears. "I see four bad-looking men. I am going to run before they see me and—maybe—swim. Good-bye."

"What in the world shall we do?" exclaimed Bud.

"I'm going to find out," declared Cub, as he dashed out of the cabin.

Hal, meanwhile, was busy again. The mysterious amateur who had persistently attempted to turn the supposed near-tragedy into a joke was spitting the Catwhisker's call again.

"Fools!" he flashed spitefully. "Goodnight."

CHAPTER VI

A Mystery and Cub's "Goat"

Cub hastened to his father and gave him a rapid narrative of events as they had been received by wireless.

"Well, that's interesting, to say the least," observed Mr. Perry with a look of curious amusement.

Cub waited a few moments for further comment, but as it was slow coming, he asked impulsively:

"What are we going to do?"

"What do you think we ought to do?" inquired the man at the wheel, looking sharply at his son.

"I don't know; I'm stumped," was the boy's reply.

"That's a frank admission. First time I've known you to admit such absolute defeat. Do you think we'd better turn about and go back home?"

"No," Cub replied with a revival of decision in his tone of voice.

"Well, shall we stop, turn to the right or left, or go ahead?"

There was a slump to indecision again. Cub looked foolish. His father was making sport of him and he did not know how to answer intelligently. In desperation, however, he replied:

"Go ahead."

"What for?" asked Mr. Perry. "Shall we dash to the rescue and face those four men, who probably are armed with pistols?"

"No, of course not. Anyway, we don't know where they are. They may be twenty-five miles from here, for all we know."

"Then we'll have to give up the search if you don't get any more messages from him," declared the boy's father.

"That's so," Cub admitted. "And if those men captured him and took him away in their boat, this affair will have to remain a mystery in our lives forever afterward."

"You'd better go back to the cabin and see if Bud and Hal got any more messages from him," suggested Mr. Perry.

"That's the only hope left," said Cub as he turned to go.

But this "last hope" proved to be vain. Bud and Hal were both still listening-in, but with little suggestion of expectancy on their countenances.

"Anything more?" inquired the tall youth, unwilling to put his question in negative form, in spite of the fact that his better judgment would have dictated it thus.

Both listeners shook their heads.

"Then that's the end of our search," Cub declared with a crestfallen and disgusted look.

"Why?" asked Bud.

"Answer the question yourself; it's easy,"

"I don't see why we should give up just because we've run up against an obstacle a little worse than any we've met before," said Hal.

"All right," Cub challenged. "Let's see what you propose to do."

"Well," Hal responded slowly; "we could go on till we found—"

He stopped and looked foolish.

"Found what?" asked Cub. "The island? How would you do that without something to guide your radio compass?"

"That's so"; Hal admitted, with another foolish look.

"It's too bad," Bud broke in, with tone well suited to his words.

"I suppose the next thing for us to do is to look for a tie-up for the night." said Hal indicating his sense of defeat by his change of subject.

"I think father is doing that now," replied Cub. "Guess I'll go and see what his idea is on that subject."

By this time the Catwhisker was several miles beyond Grindstone Island and was winding its way through a labyrinthine group to the north of Grandview. The scenery here was so enchanting that Cub and his father speedily agreed that the first convenient, unclaimed natural harbor that they discovered ought to be adopted as theirs for the night.

The season was well opened, and there were many boats on the river, so many, indeed, that it seemed strange that any live, intelligent person could be marooned on one of those islands, however vast their number, without being able to call attention to his distress. However, there were main highways in this, as in any other, semi-wilderness, and doubtless some of the by-ways were less accessible, if not less inviting and in the nature of things, less frequently visited.

This company of "rescue tourists" had motored through the Lake of the Thousand Islands before, and hence were not at a loss at any time how to find their way. The spectacle, therefore, of a hit-and-miss, crazy-quilt arrangement of long, round, high, low, green, bare islands, many of them decked with a wealth of firs, pines, tamaracks, oaks, maples, bushes and flowers, was not new to them. However, it was not long after their decision to look for a mooring place when they found an ideal cove and tied the Catwhisker to an overhanging bent, gnarled, contorted pine tree.

No camp was made on the shore, as they had no intention of remaining at this place longer than until the next break of day. All hands were pretty tired after supper, but Hal decided he must listen-in for a while before going to bed. So he donned a pair of phones and began to tune for an evening program, when a call, clear and distinct, addressed to him, suddenly held his attention.

It was from the now mysterious "V A X", the "Island Crusoe". Hal answered it and then received the following message:

"Thanks awfully for your good intentions, but I didn't need any help. Sorry to have troubled you. I did have a wager with that other fellow, but not the kind he described. It was the first big contest in the history of radio. I gave odds of four to one and am the winner. We both went to the island together and each put up an independent receiving and sending set. My part of the contest was to induce someone to come to the rescue of me as an island prisoner; his part was to head off any such rescue. He admitted I won after it was certain you were headed for us, and then we both lost our nerve and ducked. Good-bye."

Bud and Cub took the hint, from Hal's eager and almost awed manner, that something unusual was coming in through the ether and donned phones in time to catch the latter half of the message. This was sufficient to give them a clear understanding of the situation. After the "good-bye" finish, Hal made a desperate effort to hold the "Island operator" for further conversation, but could get no reply. At last he gave it up and they turned their attention to discussion of the situation.

"Well, I wonder if that's the last well hear from him," said Bud as he removed the phones from his ears, while the other two boys did likewise.

"More of a puzzle than ever, isn't it?" Cub remarked.

"Why, don't you believe the explanation he telegraphed to us?" Hal inquired.

"I do not," the tall youth replied positively.

"Why not?" Hal persisted. "Doesn't it satisfy your lordship?"

"Cut it out, Tee-hee," the alleged "lordship" ordered. "You make me sore."

"Then I'll rub on some salve."

"If you do, you'll get your fingers burnt," Cub retorted.

"I always thought you were a hot one. But that doesn't answer the question before us."

"No, because we don't know how to settle it," Cub admitted. "If we knew what we're talkin' about, we wouldn't be batting this nonsense back and forth. We can't hit the nail on the head, so we just fan the air. By the way, what did that fellow say before Bud and I began to listen-in?"

Hal reviewed the first half of the statement received by him. Then Mr. Perry, who had just returned from ashore, where he had been testing the security of the tie-up, entered the cabin.

"What's the trouble, boys?" he asked, noting the studied expression of their faces.

"No trouble, exactly," Cub replied. "Just another mystery."

"That's interesting," the yachtsman commented. "Tell me about it."

"You get my goat, dad," Cub declared.

Mr. Perry laughed.

"Why do I get your goat, Bob?" he asked.

"Because the more mystery there is floating around, the better pleased you are."

"Is that so? Well, what's the mystery now?"

"You tell 'im, Hal," requested the youth of the "goat-got affliction".

Hal did as requested. Quiet of several moments followed.

"Well?" Mr. Perry interrogated.

"Well!". repeated Cub vociferously. "Is that all you can say?"

"I'd like to return your goat, Bob, but I don't see how I can," Mr. Perry announced provokingly.

"In other words, you don't see anything startling about that fellow's last performance," Cub inferred.

"No—o, nothing startling," his father replied slowly.

"What do you make out of it, then?"

"I don't know that I make anything out of it, except a lot of nonsense."

"You think it's a joke?"

"I wouldn't call it anything but a lot of nonsense until I know more about it."

"But doesn't it make you impatient to find out what it all means?"

Cub demanded.

"No, not in the least. I got over that long ago, my son. Don't let any such habit grip you; it'll wear your nerves out, and then you won't have any lead-in to connect your antennae with your brains."

"Ha, ha, ha," laughed the man's youthful audience in chorus, even Cub appreciating the illustration.

"When did you begin to study radio, Mr. Perry?" asked Bud.

"Oh, I've been learning rapidly ever since I was thrown into the company of you hams," was the reply. "But don't let me get you off the question."

"The question—what was the question?" asked Cub, digging his fingers into his rather lengthy locks of hair.

"Mystery, wasn't it?" reminded Mr. Perry.

"Yes, that's it," Bud replied. "The mystery of the Radio Robinson Crusoe in the Lake of the Thousand Isles."

"That sounds interesting, but it's mostly a poetic, or ecstatic, jumble of words," said Mr. Perry. "And right there is the secret of many a mystery. It's clothed in a maze of language. Remove the maze, and it begins to look simple."

"Where is the maze of language in this affair?" Cub challenged.

"From what I've heard, the whole affair seems to have consisted principally of language. Now, I tell you what we'll do. We'll go to bed early and have a good sleep. In the morning, we'll shake this affair up in a sieve and see if we can't get rid of everything but the main lumps of the facts. Then we'll size them up and see what we can make of them. In my opinion, we can get at the bottom of what you choose to regard as a profound mystery."

"If you do, pa, you'll return my goat," said Cub.

"It's up to you, Bob," was his father's reply. "I've no desire to keep him in my stable."

CHAPTER VII

Returning Cub's "Goat"

In the morning after breakfast Mr. Perry called a conference on deck for the purpose of discussing "the mystery and Cub's goat", as Hal put it.

"Yes," said Bud, his sense of humor stimulated by this allusion; "all Mr. Perry has to do to return Cub's goat is to prove there isn't any mystery about the affair."

"I didn't say I was going to do that," objected the adult member of the party.

"What—return the goat or disprove the mystery?" asked Bud.

"Now you're getting facetious," broke in Cub.

"Not necessarily," objected Mr. Perry. "I didn't promise, or have in mind, to do either of those things. The fact of the matter is, a mystery represents the state or condition of mind of the person mystified. Now, I am not mystified over this affair at all; hence there is no mystery in it, so far as I am concerned."

"Then explain it to us," Bud challenged.

"Oh, no; I didn't mean I could do that."

"Then you must be mystified," Bud argued.

"Suppose you have a difficult example to do at school, and finally after working at it a long time you have to confess you can't do it—does that mean it's a mystery and you are mystified?"

This was a poser for the boys. They had never looked at a subject of this kind on any such light.

"Cub, you're the highbrow of our bunch," said Hal after some moments of puzzled silence.

"Oh, get away with that stuff," Cub protested, but, somehow, a faint glimmer of satisfaction at the "compliment" shone in his countenance.

"No, I won't, either," Hal insisted. "It's true. This thing is too much for Bud and me. You've got to settle it for us."

Cub "swelled up" a little with importance at this admission. He was sitting in a camp chair with his feet resting on the taffrail, it being a habit of his to rest his feet on something higher than his head, if possible, whenever seated. Now, however, there seemed to be a demand for superior head-work, so he lowered his feet, straightened up his back, and said:

"Well."—speaking slowly—"I don't want to get in bad with my father by trying to prove I know more than he does, but my argument would be that all of life is not arithmetic."

"Good!" exclaimed Hal, eager to defend his belief in things mysterious, and Bud signified his approval in similar manner.

"Yes, that isn't bad at all," admitted Mr. Perry, glad to have stimulated his son's mind into action. "But if we can't explain this affair with mathematics, maybe we can explain it by some other element of human education."

"What, for instance?" asked Cub. "Not by readin', 'ritin', or 'rithmetic."

"No, we'll exclude the three R's for the present, although all of them may figure in our work before it is finished."

"Well," mused Cub; "the others are history, geography, spelling— "

"Why didn't you stop with geography?" asked his father.

"Geography!" exclaimed Bud. "How can you use that to explain a mystery?"

"It depends on whether geography is involved," Mr. Perry replied. "In this case it seems to me that geography is a very important element. We may have to know considerably more about the geography of the Thousand Islands in order to solve this so-called mystery. Now, mind you, I don't mean to say that we're going to get at the bottom of this affair, but I do want to suggest that if it is to be solved by any systematic process, the first elements to be employed in the process are a little geography and a little arithmetic. With this in view, I would suggest that you get busy with your wireless outfit and see what you can find out."

The three boys gazed curiously at Cub's father and then at one another in a puzzled manner.

"Haven't I given you enough hint?" asked Mr. Perry. "I don't want to do the work myself—in fact, I couldn't if I wished to, for I can't send a wireless message; but if I could, I know exactly what I'd do."

"We might send a broadcast to all other amateurs and find out if any of them can help us," Hal suggested.

"How could they help us?" asked Bud skeptically.

"I'm sure I can't tell you," replied Mr. Perry. "But you have a dandy field to work on. All you need is a little imagination; then begin to do a little head-work, and before you know it you'll have a lead to work on. And let me add something more. There are two things in this world, which, working together, can knock a mystery into a cocked hat more successfully than anything else in the world that I know of."

"I bet I know what they are," Cub volunteered, eagerly.

"Mathematics and imagination," almost shouted Hal in a wild scramble of mind to beat Cub with the answer.

The latter cast a wrathful glance at the saucy youth who had broken in ahead of him.

"Tee-hee!" laughed Bud with fitting imitation of Hal's characteristic vocal merriment.

As for Tee-hee, that worthy individual preserved his dignity for the nonce.

"Well," laughed Mr. Perry; "You've hit the nail on the head, but I venture to say you can't explain why mathematics and imagination can put a mystery to rout."

Hal confessed he was unable to explain.

"It's too much highbrow for me," he said. "And I bet it's too much highbrow for Cub."

The latter said nothing. Evidently he was thinking hard. He leaned back in his camp chair and hoisted his feet upon the rail again.

"Well, let's quit the highbrow field and get down to business," suggested Mr. Perry. "If we're able to put this thing through along mathematical lines, I bet you boys will have enough imagination to tell me why mathematics and imagination can put any mystery on earth to rout."

"I'm goin' to get busy with the spark gap," Cub announced suddenly, as he sprang to his feet.

"You've got a big thing ahead of you, boys," announced the owner of the Catwhisker. "I venture to say there are some big surprises in store for you. For instance, you're likely to find the newspapers of the United States and Canada giving considerable space to this affair."

"How are they going to get hold of it?" asked Bud.

"There's where you're short of imagination, my boy. How many amateurs do you suppose were listening in and got the messages between you and those two radio contestants?"

"I bet there were a hundred if there was one," declared Hal.

"And were they interested?"

"Were they?" exclaimed Cub. "Every last one of 'em was wild with curiosity."

"And did they talk about it to anybody?"

"They didn't talk about anything else," Bud opined.

"And didn't you suppose some of those amateurs know some newspaper reporters?"

"We fellows all know several reporters," said Cub, with an appreciative grin.

"All right," said Mr. Perry, significantly. "Now, all I have to say to you boys is, watch the headlines whenever you get near a news stand."

The three radio boys now repaired to the cabin, while the owner of the yacht busied himself about matters of nautical interest to him on deck.

"You've got to hand it to my father for one thing," Cub declared as he seated himself near the radio table and hoisted his feet thereupon. "He sure has some imagination."

"And some mathematics, too, the way he subtracts mist from mystery every time our brains get lost in a fog," Hal added, with a self-appreciative "tee-hee."

Cub and Bud also laughed in spite of Hal's excusable self-appreciation.

"Do you know, I don't feel nearly so mystified as I did before that talk with your father began," Bud announced.

"It's the mathematics and imagination getting their work in," Cub explained with a wink.

"It sounds funny, and yet, I can't help feeling there's something to it,"

Hal remarked.

"Well," said Cub, bringing his feet down from the table with enough noise to rivet a conclusion; "you may call it addition, or subtraction, or multiplication, or division, or algebra, or geometry, or trigonometry, or calculus—does that complete the list?—I'm going to make my imagination leap across the spark gap; so here goes."

He snapped the aerial switch into sending, began to "jiggle" the key alphabetically, and the spark leaped with successive spits across the gap.

"Cub's got his goat back," Hal remarked with a knowing look at Bud.

The latter grinned and nodded his concurrence.

CHAPTER VIII

Mathematics or Geography?

But the morning proved to be a poor time for communication by radio for two reasons. First, the atmosphere was warm, a poor condition for the transmission of ether waves, and after all, night time is the ideal season for such doings. Second, comparatively few amateurs were sitting in at this time of the day, although vacation had arrived and closed the schoolhouse doors.

Cub kept up his efforts for an hour, with virtually no success. Although he succeeded in communicating with half a dozen "hams", only one of them had listened-in to any of the messages that passed between the Catwhisker boys and the two Canadian radio contestants, and he was able to throw no light on the "mystery". At last he gave it up for the time being, and joined the other Catwhiskerites on deck for a period of sightseeing enjoyment.

They cruised about among the islands most of the day, stopping here and there to inspect some apparently unclaimed scene of enchantment, or visiting various places exploited for gain by private interests as centers of entertainment and recreation. They circumnavigated Wellesly Island, making short stops at several points of interest and at about 4:30 p.m. tied up in a quiet shelter overhung by a low-limbed tamarack and cast their baited fishhooks into the water for a "brain-food" supper. This was not more than half a mile from the tie-up where they passed their first night in the Thousand Islands. The finny fellows bit greedily and in a short time they had enough black bass and pickerel to feed a party twice the size of theirs.

After supper all repaired to the cabin, and the boys donned phones, while Cub started a broadcasting campaign in search of information regarding the two Canadian wireless contestants, who seemed to have made a trio of monkeys out of the three radio motor-boat boys.

"I haven't much idea what kind of questions to ask or what kind of answers to expect," he said to his companions; "but here goes my best guess."

He had selected an intermission period in the atmosphere when the big broadcasting stations were quiet, and then gave the general call and sent out the following:

"I want help to identify and locate an amateur who figured in mysterious radio affair in last two days. He said his name was Raymond Flood, that he lived in Kingston, that his call was V A X, and that he was marooned on island in St. Lawrence River. Can anybody help me? Call A V L."

Immediately three amateurs, two in Canada and one in New York State, clamored for a hearing. Cub wrote down their calls and then took on the one in Kingston first.

"There is no such amateur in Kingston," the latter announced. "I know them all here. V A X is held by somebody in Port Hope. I listened-in to a lot of that stuff and called up three amateurs in Port Hope. I learned that A V L is Alvin Baker who is attending Edwards College."

"Why, he's my cousin!"

This exclamation from Hal created a real sensation in the cabin of the Catwhisker. Meanwhile Bud had been taking the message down longhand in order to preserve a record of the investigation, so that Mr. Perry, who read as the boys wrote, got the progress of events about as rapidly as did the three youthful experts. It is needless to say that he was as much astonished as were his boy companions.

But there was no time now for a discussion of family relationship. After a round of gasps and exclamations, they got down again to the business of their radio investigation.

That was about the extent of the information that the Kingston amateur was able to communicate to them, except that he had been an interested listener-in to much of the code conversations between the would-be rescuers and the two very strange radio contestants. He, however, promised to make further inquiries and to call them again if he learned anything that might be of interest to them.

"Well, dad, it looks as if you were right when you told us how to go about to solve this mystery," Cub remarked as he dash-and-dotted a "G N" (good night) to the Kingston amateur.

"You mean problem," reminded Mr. Perry with a smile.

"Well, maybe,—I won't dispute your word since your idea has proved so brilliant thus far—but I can't see the mathematics yet."

"Nor the geography?"

"Well, yes; it took us from Kingston to Port Hope and from there to Edwards College," Cub admitted. "I suppose there's a little geography in that."

"Remember this, that mathematics isn't all figures," said the operator's father. "Keep that in mind, and maybe it'll be worth something to you before we're through with this affair."

"How does the discovery of my cousin come in?" Hal inquired. "Is that geography or mathematics?"

"Do you mean that, Hal?" asked Bud wonderingly. "You don't mean that fellow is really your cousin?"

"I surely do, if he's Alvin Baker. You know my folks used to live in Canada. And don't you remember that my cousin Al visited us three years ago with his father and mother? He wrote to me several times from Edwards College, but I didn't know he had a wireless set, and I suppose he didn't know I had one."

"Well, it makes the hunt more interesting, anyway," said Cub. "But let's not waste any more time. Here goes again."

He called the other Canadian amateur on his list of three and learned from him that many wireless boys had followed the course of the rescue boat with their receiving outfits. From him Cub got the calls of four of these interested boys. Then he called the third on his original list, but all the information the latter was able to give was that a metropolitan morning newspaper carried a column "story" on the front page about the Thousand Island Crusoe and the rescue boat from Oswego.

"You're right again, dad," said Cub, with a grim grin of subdued wonder and eagerness.

"I shouldn't be a bit surprised to find that the Associated Press has chartered a boat and is following us," declared Mr. Perry.

"Would that be mathematics or geography?" asked Bud.

"It would be imagination," replied Mr. Perry with a keen smile. "But, say, Cub, don't you think you've grabbed off enough glory for yourself? Give your friends a chance to win some honors."

"Right you are, dad," returned the boy at the key, rising and removing the phones from his ears. "Hal, you call half this list and then let Bud call the rest"

It was well for the sake of a distribution of honors that this course was taken, for a thrilling surprise was in store for them in response to the next call.

CHAPTER IX

The Radio Diagram

As good fortune decreed, Hal found Number One in the new list sitting in and listening for anything interesting in the ether. It required only a few short sentences to acquaint this amateur with the object of the Catwhisker's search.

"I can tell you just how to find those fellows," he replied. "I listened-in to the best line of detective work on that subject you ever heard of. Sherlock Holmes isn't in it there."

"Hooray!" shouted Bud, as he finished jotting down the last sentence.

"There are three amateurs, one in Clayton, N.Y., one in Rockport and one in Gananoque, Ontario, who have radio compasses and they worked together to locate the fellow on the island," continued the informant with the eagerness of fraternal interest and generosity. "I will give you their calls— "

The message was interrupted by a strong spark, which could not be ignored. Sender Number one stopped sending, and Hal gave ear to the new message.

"I will save you the trouble," read the dots and dashes evidently addressed to the operator he had just "crowded out," "I am at Rockport and am one of the three radio compass boys referred to. I can supply the dope right now."

Hal threw over the aerial switch and flashed the one word "Shoot!" Then he swung back again and all three boys listened eagerly.

"Have you a good map of the Thousand Island region?" inquired the loop aerial operator.

"Yes," Hal replied.

"Well, take these directions and then draw the line on the map. Draw one line from Clayton, N.Y., northeast, 47-1/2 degrees from perpendicular; another from Rockport, Ontario, southeast, 11 degrees from perpendicular; another from Gananoque, southeast, 76 degrees from perpendicular. The intersection of those lines will indicate the island those messages came from."

"He was on an island, was he?" asked Hal.

"Sure, or on a boat," was the reply. "He could not have been on the mainland. We were careful and could not have been more than a mile off in our reckoning. All three of us hit it the same."

"Where was the fellow who tried to head us off?" asked Hal.

"When?"

"At any time."

"We located him at various points along the river. No doubt he was on a boat up to the very last when the two were very near together."

"Where was the island operator when he sent his last message? Did you get the one in which he confessed the affair was a hoax?"

"Yes. But he did not send that message. It was sent by the other fellow."

"How do you know?"

"That was plain. Did you not notice his peculiar manner of sending? All three of us noticed that."

"Did you pick up any more from them since then?"

"Not a dot."

Hal then asked the obliging amateur to indicate as nearly as possible the location of the island from which the messages came. The latter did as requested, and Hal marked the point on the chart of the St. Lawrence River carried by the Catwhisker. This closed the wireless interview. Hal promised to report back to the Rockport amateur any further developments of interest and tapped "goodnight" with his key.

"Well, your two main points have been proved, Mr. Perry," Bud announced as all three boys removed the receivers from their ears.

"What are they?" asked the man thus addressed.

"Mathematics and geography."

Mr. Perry smiled.

"Yes," he said "I could hardly have hoped for so remarkable a demonstration of my theory. You boys have solved the geography of this problem with the aid of some very clever mathematics. But what branch of mathematics is it?"

"We didn't do it ourselves," Hal reminded. "It was those three amateurs with their loop aerials."

"Wasn't it more mechanical than mathematical?" Cub inquired meditatively.

"Those radio compasses make me think of a surveyor's instrument."

"Oh, pshaw, my boy, don't spoil everything," pleaded the last speaker's father. "I'm afraid you've missed the big point. Mathematics is the biggest factor in all mechanics. Bud, I thought from the way you spoke that you grasped the situation completely. Can't you help Bob and Hal out? By means of what branch of mathematics was that island of our Canadian Crusoe located?"

"Geometry," replied Bud confidently.

Cub snapped his finger with an impatient jerk of his long right arm.

"Of course!" he exclaimed in disgust. "Every branch of mathematics I ever heard of, except geometry, went buzzing through my head. I was trying to recall something in algebra that would fit this case."

"Oh, Cub," laughed Hal; "algebra is all x's and y's and z's over z's and y's and x's,"

"I admit I'm a chump," Cub grinned with a shrug of self-commiseration; "but say, let's draw those geometrical lines on our chart and see if we get the same result those radio compass fellows got."

Cub produced the chart and a hand-book diagram of a mariner's compass about three inches in diameter. Fortunately the chart was made of thin, vellum-like paper, almost transparent, so that when laid over the diagram, the minute points of the compass, indicated with clear black lines, could be seen through. First the dot representing the town of Clayton was placed over the point at the center of the compass, with the north and south line of the compass exactly coinciding with the meridian of the town. Then Cub traced on the chart lightly with a pencil the 47-1/2-degree northeast line of the compass. Next he performed a similar operation with the center of the diagram over Rockport and next with the center of the diagram over Gananoque, following instructions in each of these cases with reference to the direction lines to be drawn. The result was that the intersection of the three lines was at approximately the point indicated by the Rockport amateur.

"Now we're ready to continue our search," Cub announced.

"That's pretty good progress, I must say," Bud declared; "but here's a new question to get us into trouble again."

"Oh, for goodness sake, don't," pleaded Cub. "You've had your example of what my mathematical dad can do with such foolish creatures."

"Let him express his doubt," suggested Mr. Perry with a smile; "for, if a man must doubt, he'd better shout than smother his ideas in a skeptic pout."

"Yes, get it off your chest, Bud, and then take your medicine," advised Hal.

"Well, suppose we find the island and nobody there, how are we going to know it's the right one?"

This hit the other two boys pretty hard. The possibility of such a situation had not occurred to either of them. However, Cub preferred to take it in lighter vein, for he replied:

"By his footprints on the sandy beach. You mustn't have a Crusoe Island without some footprints, you know."

"The trouble is you're anticipating too rapidly, Bud," Mr. Perry advised.

"Columbus would never have discovered America in that frame of mind."

"All right, I'll change the frame," said Bud. "We'll just go ahead and see what we shall see."

"We've got to go ahead if Hal's cousin is in peril," declared Cub.

"Do you really believe the Crusoe boy is your cousin, Hal?" asked Bud.

"Of course that's hard to believe, but the evidence points in that direction," Hal replied.

"At least if he is your cousin, we know now that he wasn't making monkeys out of us, as that last message, supposed to come from him, made it appear he was doing," Cub admitted.

"Yes," put in Mr. Perry; "it looks now as if he was telling a straight story all along."

"If that's true, then he's probably in serious trouble right now," said

Hal.

"Probably a prisoner in the hands of robbers, if not worse," Bud supplemented.

"Let's go to bed at once and get a good night's rest so that we will be in condition to put forth our best efforts to find him and rescue him in the morning," proposed Mr. Perry.

This proposal met with indorsement from all, and in a short time they were in their berths, employing their best skill to induce sleep under condition of much mental excitement.

CHAPTER X

The Island-Surrounded Island

Early next morning the Catwhisker left its mooring under the tamarack and started on the new search for the "Canadian Crusoe's" island.

Guided by the "mathematical chart" prepared with the directions given by the radio-compass amateur, the crew of the motor boat had little difficulty in finding the approximate location of the island prison; but when arrived there, they realized that considerable work was still before them, for they were in the midst of a veritable sea of islands, varying in size from a few car-loads of stone and earth to several acres in extent.

"Well, how are we goin' to begin?" asked Hal as Cub stopped the engine in a pond-like expanse, surrounded by a more or less regular rim of islands.

"The first thing to do, I should say is to make the best possible reckoning of our bearings and then try to fix the point of intersection of those three lines indicated by the radio compasses," said Mr. Perry.

"That's right," Cub agreed. "We mustn't forget our mathematics."

"It seems to me that we ought to be able to pick this place on the chart," Bud suggested.

"Yes, especially if we keep in mind the location of some other landmarks, or watermarks, that we passed in the last half or three-quarters of an hour in getting here," said Hal.

Cub produced the chart, and the study of locations and island arrangements began. As indicated by expectations in the course of their discussion, they were able to locate a few of the larger islands and with these as bases for further reckoning, they at last picked out what seemed to be the point of intersection of the three pencil lines on the chart. This necessitated a little more cruising about, but within an hour after their first stop they completed their reckoning.

"There's the island that seems to come nearest to the intersection," said Mr. Perry, pointing toward an abrupt elevation, a hundred yards long and half as wide and covered with bushes and a few small trees; "but it doesn't seem to answer the description very well. No other islands near it."

"I don't see how anybody could be marooned on that place with boats passing back and forth near it every hour of the day," Hal commented skeptically.

"Neither do I," Bud agreed.

"Well, let's do our work thoroughly anyway," Mr. Perry suggested.

"Shall we go ashore and look that place over?" asked Hal.

"Sure."

"But what do you expect to find?" Cub inquired.

"I don't expect to find anything. I had no expectation when I suggested that you boys canvass the radio field for information to clear up what you chose to call a mystery. I had no idea what might turn up as a result of such canvass, but I know it was about the only thing for you to do to start a move in the desired direction."

"And something sure did move," Hal remarked appreciatively.

"Well, let's run around this island and find a landing place," Cub proposed.

The run was made, with Cub in charge of the wheel and engine controls.

They circumnavigated the island with unsatisfactory result.

"That settles it," Bud declared. "If San Salvador had been like that,

Columbus would have made his first landing somewhere else!"

"Robinson Crusoe would never have found any footprints in the sand there," Hal declared.

"Yes, we'll give it up for the time being," Mr. Perry declared. "We won't try to scale any perpendicular banks, fifteen or twenty feet high, at least, not to begin with."

"I tell you what we ought to do," Hal volunteered next. "Let's accept this island as the center of probability."

"What in thunder is that?" Cub demanded.

"That's a good one on you, son," laughed the latter's father. "I thought you were the highbrow of your bunch; but here's our subtle Tee-hee putting a bit of clever phraseology over on you."

"Oh, I know what he means," Cub rejoined with a panicky haste to recover lost prestige. "I was just giving him a dig. He's forever giving me one, whenever I come along with anything of that kind."

"It indicates that his mind is maturing rapidly," said Mr. Perry. "All right, Hal, we'll accept this island as a center of probability—what next?"

"Why, let's cruise around about half a mile in all directions and pick out those islands that look as if they might have concealed a prisoner from view of passing boats."

"That's a good suggestion," said Mr. Perry. "Bob, start the boat again."

The inspection required about an hour, at the end of which they compared notes and found that their island inventory disclosed the following conditions:

Three possible places of concealment for the "Canadian Crusoe" had been discovered. Two were small islands a short distance from each other in a region of shallows and more or less hidden by rows of long slim islands. No boat of greater draught than a canoe could make its way through the intervening passages. In other words, these islands were virtually isolated from all river traffic. The other possible place of concealment was an island about five acres in extent, completely hemmed in by a group of other islands, which were so overrun with rampant vegetation, including bushes and trees, as to conceal the inner isle from any but the most scrutinizing vision.

"That is the place we want to explore first," announced Mr. Perry as reference was made to this retreat in the check-up.

"I agree with you," Bud declared. "If the prisoner left any traces behind him at all, we're likely to find them on that island in there."

"Is there any way we can get in?" Hal inquired. "Too bad we haven't a small rowboat or canoe with us."

"We'll investigate and see what we can find in the way of a water passage into the interior," Mr. Perry announced.

"That means a little more circumnavigating," Bud inferred.

"Right you are," said Cub. "Me to the pilot house again."

Accordingly he resumed his position at the wheel and the boat was put in motion again. His father followed him and cautioned him against too much speed in such places.

Slowly the Catwhisker crept around the island-surrounded island until they discovered a passage somewhat wider and apparently deeper than others they had seen thus far in the outer rim.

"It looks as if we might get through there," suggested Hal. He and Bud had followed into the pilot house soon after Cub and his father repaired to that place.

"It does look a little that way," replied Mr. Perry.

"We might creep in there slowly, and if we find the passage obstructed so as to block our way, we could back out," Hal continued.

"We have some long fender poles," Cub amended. "We could feel our way with them and probably keep out of serious trouble."

"All right, let's make the attempt," said Mr. Perry. "I'd very much like to get in there with this boat."

Cub started the engine and the Catwhisker began slowly to nose its way through the passage. In a few minutes the little craft was alongside a ledge of rock that projected as a sort of forehead from the top of a perpendicular short front, and the pilot brought her to a full stop.

CHAPTER XI

The Deserted Camp

Both the inner island and the surrounding rim of elongated isles were covered with a thick growth of trees and bushes, a condition that caused Hal to exclaim:

"I bet this is the place."

"What makes you so certain of that?" inquired Mr. Perry, looking sharply at the boy.

"Because it's an ideal place for a Crusoe to be hidden so that passing ships could not see him," Hal replied.

"But might he not swim over to one of these surrounding islands and attract attention from there?"

"Yes, if there's a place to get ashore after swimming across," said Cub.

"There's nothing but high steep banks all along here, so far as I can see," Bud remarked.

"That's a good line of observation," was Mr. Perry's commendation. "Now, let's explore this island and see if your points are well taken."

Even the landing at which the boat now rested was not particularly attractive as such at first view because of a rather difficult climb between it and the main level of the island. However, all the members of the band of "Crusoe hunters" were good climbers and they soon made their way up the stony steep to the surface land level.

"It's funny somebody hasn't picked this place as a site for a summer home," Mr. Perry remarked as he took a hurried view of his surroundings.

"The trouble is it doesn't look like a very interesting place from a view out on the river, and there are hundreds of islands to choose from," said Cub.

"Yes, I suppose so," his father agreed; "but in my opinion the place deserves a second look-over. I'm going to keep it in mind as a future prospect."

"We'll have to put up a radio station here then," said Cub.

"Oh, sure, we can't do without that wherever we go now-a-days," his father replied.

They skirted the entire shore of the island and found Bud's suggestion regarding high, steep banks to be true in every quarter. Not another practical landing place, except with derrick or rope ladder, was discovered. They estimated the island to be about five acres in extent.

"Well, we haven't found much evidence yet, indicating that this is the place we were looking for," Cub remarked as they arrived back at the starting point of their exploration.

"I suppose the next thing for us to do is to explore the interior of the island, and then perhaps we'll be in a position to form some sort of conclusion," said Mr. Perry.

"All right, let's finish this job as soon as possible," Bud proposed, as he started toward a thicket of bushes and small trees a few yards from the landing place.

All being in harmony with this plan, there was a general move toward the interior. The thicket, however, proved to be only about twenty feet in depth, and beyond this was a clear area a quarter of an acre in extent.

"Somebody's had a camp here not many days ago," Cub announced, as he pressed forward eagerly toward the center of the open area.

"Yes, and a tent has stood right here," said Mr. Perry, indicating several guy-rope stakes driven in the ground.

"Whoever it was didn't leave more than a day or two ago," Hal declared.

"See how the grass is tramped down around here?"

"What's this?" exclaimed Bud as he ran back toward the thicket through which they had passed and picked up a pole about ten feet long and two inches thick.

Mr. Perry and the other two boys rushed forward and made an eager examination of Bud's discovery.

"This looks interesting," said Bud significantly as he called attention to several worn places at both ends and the middle of the pole, as if with iron rings or wire held close around it under a strain.

"There's another just like this one over there," cried Hal, suddenly darting forward toward a slender pine tree about a hundred feet away and standing a short distance out from the thicket border of the open area.

Mr. Perry, Cub, and Bud rushed after Hal, who picked up, under the pine tree, a pole almost the exact duplicate of the one found by Bud. After a careful examination of them both, Mr. Perry announced:

"It looks to me, boys, as if you had discovered the spreaders of a demolished aerial."

"No doubt of it," Hal agreed. "Somebody used this tree and that one over there as masts of an aerial."

"But trees are not supposed to be good for aerial masts," Bud objected.

"They're all right if you have your insulation well out beyond the branches," said Cub.

"Yes, that's true," Bud admitted. "And look up there—see that wire? The fellow who took down this aerial didn't do his work very well."

All looked up in the tree and saw a wire hanging down among the branches and appearing to be attached at the farther end near the top of the pine.

"It was probably done in a hurry," Mr. Perry observed.

"And that is one more point to the argument that this is the island we were looking for," said Bud.

"Yes, but the fellow we came to rescue is gone and left no trace where he's gone to," added Cub.

"Still, don't you think the search has been worth while?" the latter's father inquired.

"I do," put in Hal, who had been noticeably quiet and meditative since the last very important discovery. "This makes it look as if that last distress message we got from the island was no fake affair?"

"Why?" asked Bud.

"Why!" flashed Hal. "It's plain enough to me. Those four fellows, he said were coming to attack him, probably overpowered him and swept away his camp, radio outfit, and all."

"And what did they do with him?" demanded Cub, eager for the last chapter of the plot.

Hal seemed about to make answer to this question, but something of the nature of a "lump in his throat" checked his utterance. His friends read his mind without difficulty.

"Never mind, Hal," said Cub with his bravest effort at consolation; "if the prisoner on this island was your cousin, we'll follow those enemies of his to the end of the world and make them give him up, won't we, dad?"

"Don't you worry too much over this affair, Hal," urged Mr. Perry by way of response to his son's extravagant assurance. "If the person you got those messages from was your cousin, I don't believe the fellows who were after him had reason to do him any serious harm. But you may be sure that we will not leave a stone unturned in an effort to solve this—this—"

"Mystery," suggested Cub mischievously grasping at the opportunity to give his father a good-natured dig.

"Call it what you wish," smiled Mr. Perry. "But under any name you may be pleased to style this problem, we are going to go after it with some more mathematics—"

"And geography," interposed Cub.

"Yes, and geography, and you boys know what success we have had with mathematics and geography in this search of ours thus far. Now, meanwhile, I'm going to make a new suggestion which I hope you boys will look upon with favor. Let's establish a camp of our own right here on the spot where the Canadian Crusoe had his camp."

CHAPTER XII

Hal's Discovery

The boys were delighted with the suggestion of Mr. Perry that they establish a camp on the island and needed no urging to begin work on the project. With true outing instinct they had come prepared for just such an emergency as this. They had brought with them a tent large enough for four and a complete set of camp tools, including spade, shovel, axe, pickaxe, hatchet, saw, hammer, and nails.

Returning to the Catwhisker, they hauled all these supplies out on deck preparatory to taking them ashore.

"Let's make a better ascent up this steep bank before we carry these things up," Mr. Perry proposed. "It's quite a climb, as it is, without a load in our arms to hamper us."

"Only one person can work at a time to any advantage," Bud suggested.

"That's true," replied the director of the expedition. "But we can work in rapid shifts and finish this job quickly. I'll take the first trick and make things fly for about fifteen minutes, and then one of you can take my place."

With these words, he stripped off his coat, seized the pickaxe and shovel and stepped over the side of the boat onto the landing ledge. Then he began a vigorous attack on the steep incline between the ledge and the land level above.

The task consumed a little more than an hour of speed labor, and by that time it was after one o'clock and each of the hillside stairway builders had worked up a very healthy appetite. So they prepared and ate luncheon on board the yacht, and then began the work of moving tent and other supplies to the site selected for their camp. By the time this was done and the tent pitched, it was 3 o'clock.

"Now, what next?" asked Cub as he sat down on a camp chair after the last guy rope had been drawn taut and fastened securely to its peg. "It seems to me that it's about time for another pow-wow of the Catwhiskerites."

"I agree with you, Bob," said his father, also unfolding a camp chair and sitting down, followed by similar action on the part of the other two boys.

"Well, what's the question?" asked Bud.

"I'll offer a question if somebody'll take the chair and preside," Hal volunteered.

"All right," Bud agreed. "You act as chairman, Mr. Perry."

"I am elected by Bud, there being no opposition," announced the owner of the Catwhisker. "Now, what is the question, Hal?"

"I'll put it this way," the latter replied: "Resolved, that mathematics is more useful to a detective than a flashlight or a skeleton key."

"That isn't half-bad at all," declared Cub in the midst of general laughter and applause. "The main trouble is that we can't find anybody on this island to take the other side of the question."

"Very well," ruled the chair; "this question being decided in favor of the affirmative, we will now proceed to the next."

"Which is as follows," Bud announced; "to-wit, why have we established our camp on this island, how long are we going to remain here, and what shall we do while here?"

"Now, we're getting down to business," said Cub. "But that's a composite question. First, why are we here?"

"We're here because we're here," Hal replied solemnly.

"The chair is willing to accept that as a good and valid reason provided other collateral questions are answered satisfactorily," Mr. Perry announced.

"Next question, how long are we going to stay here?" Cub continued.

"I should say we will stay here until we find a reason for moving on to the next place," said Bud.

"Another excellent answer and fully supporting answer number one," Mr. Perry announced. "Now, for an answer to question number three—What shall we do while here?"

"I'll answer that," said Cub; "well fish, cook, eat, sleep, explore and keep our eyes peeled."

"Peeled for what?" asked Hal.

"More mathematical evidence."

"Good!" exclaimed Bud. "We mustn't lose sight of the purpose of this expedition. If our radio Crusoe is really Hal's cousin, we're bound by the ties of friendship to stick to our task till it's finished."

"Very well," said the chair. "Having settled the question of general policy, let's get down to some more detail. What shall we do next?"

"Complete our exploration of the islands," said Cub. "There's no telling what we may find."

"Now, you're beginning to look at things the way your father does," put in Hal shrewdly.

"How's that?" Cub inquired.

"Why you're willing to look for a trail. I'm not saying you were any worse than Bud and I were before we got started on this hunt. We just stumbled on a trail to begin with, but when we lost it we didn't know what to do next until your father told us it was up to us to scout around and find it again."

"Yes, that's right," Cub admitted. "We scouted around in the air and found the trail that brought us here."

"Moral: Whenever at a loss, do some broadcasting," suggested Mr. Perry.

"Right," declared Bud; "Now the thing for us to do is some physical broadcasting on this island."

"In other words, we'll all go in different directions and examine every square foot of this island," Cub inferred.

"Exactly," assented Mr. Perry. "It ought not to take very long. There are only about five acres here, although the place is pretty well covered with bushes and trees."

Without further ado they separated toward different points of the compass. It was indeed a random exploration, well characterized as something of a "broadcast," but the task was well executed by all. They had no definite expectation in view, and hence they had to content themselves with examining every physical feature as a naturalist or a topographer, perchance, would look for the feature demands of his specialty, and in about half an hour reconvened in front of their tent. Hal was the only person present with a look of excitement or eagerness on his face, and consequently the general interest of the others was directed toward him.

"You've found something, I know, Hal," Bud declared. "You came running through the bushes as if you were chased by a catamount or else you had something on your mind that threatened to burst your cranium."

"I didn't meet a catamount," replied the boy to whom these remarks were addressed; "but I did find something that excited me very much. I've learned two important things."

"What are they?" Cub demanded.

"I've learned the name of this island and made sure of the name of the person we came here to find."

"You don't say!" Cub exclaimed. "I don't see how the name of this island can mean anything to us, but we should be very glad to know who the fellow is that we came here to find."

"Well, the name of this island is important, or at least interesting," Hal returned; "and I am going to give you that first. It is Friday Island and was given that name by the Robinson Crusoe who was marooned here because he landed here last Friday. Now, I'll tell you the other important item. The fellow who was marooned with a wireless outfit was no other person than my cousin as I suspected. And I have learned why he was marooned here."

"Why?" demanded Hal's three companions in chorus.

"Because he was a college freshman and some of the upper classmen had it in for him and they simply strong-armed him, captured him, and brought him here to haze him."

Every one of Hal's three companions gasped with astonishment. The possibilities of such an explanation of this strange "radio-island affair" had never occurred to one of them.

CHAPTER XIII

"Robinson Crusoe's" Diary

"How in the world did you find that out?"

"Who told you all o' that?"

"Where is your cousin now?"

These questions and others of like character were fired at Hal in rapid succession, indicating the eagerness of all the members of his audience for more light on the subject. As for Hal, he was moved by conflicting emotions, which puzzled his friends considerably at first. He did not burst forth with a storm of replies, a thing that he might well have done consistently with boy nature. He seemed to be meditating how to begin, as if there was so much on his mind he did not know what to say first.

In reality, although this confusion of ideas probably had something to do with his momentary silence following the storm of questions rained at him, Hal was much elated with the good fortunc that had thrown some remarkable information into his possession; still, he was deeply concerned over the possible fate of his cousin. It was the latter concern, no doubt, that tempered and held in check his jubilation over his discovery.

"I think, Mr. Perry, you will admit now that there is such a thing as a mystery," he said.

"Why?" inquired the individual at whom this remark was directed.

"No, I am merely very curious," replied Mr. Perry, with a smile.

"Oh, hurry up, Hal, and tell us what this means," urged Cub impatiently. "What's the use o' keepin' us guessing all this time. Bud and I'll admit we're mystified."

"Yes," grinned Mr. Perry; "you'd better hurry up and enlighten us, or

I'll have to drag the secret out of you with mathematics."

"Addition or subtraction," asked Hal.

"Extraction," replied "the man who couldn't be mystified" with significant emphasis on the "ex".

Laughter followed this quip, the levity of which caused Hal to feel more like "loosening up".

"Well," said the latter, producing a small leather-back notebook from one of his pockets; "here is the secret of my information."

"Where did you get that?" Cub demanded.

"I found it."

"Where—not here?"

"Yes, on this island. It's a diary of my cousin, beginning with the time he was left here by a bunch of college hazers."

"Does it give any hint where he is now, Hal?" inquired Mr. Perry.

"I don't think so," replied the boy with the notebook. "I ran my eye through it hurriedly, but didn't have time to read it all. If you'll sit down and listen, I'll read it to you from the beginning."

All being agreeable to this proposition, they seated themselves on camp chairs in front of the tent and Hal began as follows:

"First, I'll begin by telling you where I found this book. I'll take you back to the spot after I've finished reading. Before I found this book, I discovered a sign, or notice, written on a piece of paper and pinned to the trunk of a tree about four feet from the ground. On that paper was written with lead pencil these words under date of last Friday:

"'I Alvin Baker, a student at Edwards College, hereby name this island Friday island, because I was marooned here alone, like Robinson Crusoe, on Friday, June 9, 1922.'"

"I'd like to make the acquaintance of that boy," said Mr. Perry warmly. "He has both imagination and a sense of humor in the midst of adversity."

"Naturally I began to look about me for some trace of the person who had pinned the notice on the tree," Hal continued. "I was standing in an open space about thirty feet in diameter. The tree on which this notice was pinned is at the edge of that space. There are a few small bushes here and there in the open, but the ground there is covered with long coarse grass. The first thing that attracted my attention, as I began to look about me was the fact that the grass was trampled down over a considerable area. I examined it carefully and while doing so found this notebook in the grass. It didn't take me long after that to reach the conclusion that Cousin Alvin had been attacked by somebody and in the struggle lost this notebook out of his pocket."

"It was probably the four ugly looking men he said were coming ashore when he sent his last distress message to us," Cub inferred.

"I wonder why he didn't tell us the truth," Bud put in. "Why didn't he tell us he was being hazed by some college boys?"

"He explains that in his diary," Hal replied. "Now listen and I'll read the first entry."

Hal's injunction being met with quiet, eager attention, he read as follows:

"Friday, June 9, 1922. Last night while I was walking through the grove of trees near the campus of Edwards College, I was attacked and overpowered by several sophomores, who slipped a bag over my head and carried me to a motor-boat moored a short distance away. They tried to conceal their identity, but I recognized the voices of Jerry Kerry and Buck Hardmaster. They kept me a helpless prisoner, with arms and legs bound and eyes bandaged, in the cabin for several hours, during which I could feel the boat constantly on the move. About 3 o'clock in the morning I was carried ashore on this island. My hands were untied, and then I could hear my captors hurrying away. I removed the bandage from my eyes and with my pocket-knife cut the rope around my ankles. It was too dark yet to see anything distinctly, so I had to wait for break of day before doing anything. An hour later I discovered near the landing place a considerable layout of supplies and equipment most of which I recognized as my own property. Then I recalled that one of my captors had thrust something into one of my pockets just before they took me ashore and I put my hand into that pocket and drew out an envelope that I knew I had not put there. In the envelope I found a typewritten note, which read as follows:

"'Alvin Baker, you have succeeded during all of your freshman year to date in frustrating every attempt to haze you and have boasted that there was no "gang" of boys at Edwards smart enough to do the trick. We are now performing the trick in a manner that ought to convince you that such a boast is the freshest of freshman folly. We raided your room and took therefrom your radio sending and receiving outfit, and have added thereto necessary equipment for erecting an aerial. This we leave with you in order that you may summon help through the atmosphere. Meanwhile, you may comfort yourself with the distinction of being the first college freshman ever given a radio hazing. Now, put up your aerial and send out a message for help. Radio is your only hope. Nobody ever stops at this island and it is impossible for passing vessels to see any signal of distress you may devise. If you are too proud to admit defeat and refuse to send out a broadcast for help, you must remain here two weeks, at the end of which time you will be captured again after dark, bound and blindfolded, and taken back to the mainland and released. The identity of the persons responsible for your defeat you will never be able to discover. Enough canned food has been left with you to keep body and soul together a week. At the end of that time, if you have failed to effect your own rescue by radio, more canned food will be left here for you. We are leaving also a tent, a few camp utensils, matches, and fishing tackle. You must drink river water. Now prove yourself as big as your boast.'

"I decided to defeat those fellows, if possible, by getting away from the island without broadcasting an admission that I had been marooned by sophomore hazers. So I pitched the tent and then constructed an aerial out of material supplied by them and began to broadcast messages of distress, saying that I had been marooned by river thieves who had stolen my boat. But soon I found that there was someone 'in the air' who was determined to defeat this purpose. It is now 11 p.m., and he seems to have been successful in his attempts to make it appear that I am a faker. Nobody has offered to come to my rescue."

Saturday's entry in the diary opened as follows:

"Last night, between 2 and 3 a.m., I was awakened by a slight noise outside near the tent. I stole cautiously to the entrance and peered out. It was a bright moonlight night and in front of the tent I saw two men apparently examining the camp with much curiosity or evil intent, perhaps both. Evidently they saw me watching them, for they suddenly turned and fled. I followed them cautiously and saw them get into a power boat and motor away. I called to them, explaining my situation and offering to pay them if they would take me away from the island, but they gave me no answer. Probably they were river thieves and the boat they had was stolen."

CHAPTER XIV

More Light and More Mystery

The next two days, Saturday and Sunday, were devoted by the island prisoner to the sending out of further calls, for help, and these calls were met by a campaign of ridicule, similar to that begun by his nemesis on the first day of his imprisonment, according to the diary read by Hal to his companions. A few listeners-in indicated a willingness to come to his rescue, in spite of the plausible ridicule from anonymous source, but when asked where he was imprisoned, ignorance on that subject frustrated all good intentions along that line until his S O S reached Cub at the latter's home on the following Monday.

"I tried to make this mysterious enemy of mine identify himself," wrote the diarist under Saturday date; "but he professed to have a wager posted against me which bound us both to secrecy. This caught me in the solar plexus of my conscience, for I was broadcasting my appeals for help under a false identity. Two or three amateurs looked me up under the name, call, and address that I gave and then broadcast a denunciation of me. It begins to look as if my hazers are going to win a full revenge for the way I laughed at them at college. This day's experience has convinced me that I am in bad throughout the radio atmosphere. It begins to look as if I am up against it and will have to stay here the full two weeks to which those hazing kidnappers of mine sentenced one. I wonder if they will make the term longer because I resorted to the method I have pursued thus far in order to avoid admitting that I had been hazed. Well, I have this consolation, anyway, that they have to pay for my food as long as I am here. They had to furnish me a tent also."

"Caught half a dozen fish today and named this place Friday island because of the day, or night, I was brought here and my subsequent Robinson Crusoe experiences," began the entry for Monday.

Then followed a gleeful memorandum of his apparent success in interesting Cub Perry with an account of his predicament, in spite of the efforts of his radio nemesis to prove him a trifler with the truth. Tuesday's entry closed with a notation of the announcement from Cub that the Catwhisker was about to start on a rescue trip from Oswego to the Lake of the Thousand Islands and would endeavor to find him by radio compass.

"The situation is cleared up very much," Mr. Perry remarked after Hal had finished reading the diary. "The chief problem now remaining to be solved is, what became of your cousin?"

"In other words, that's the mystery before us," said Bud, with a twinkle of fun in his eyes.

"Call it what you will," smiled Mr. Perry. "But it doesn't strike me as in the least mysterious. Evidently he was taken away from this island by the fellows who put him here."

"And what did they do with him?" was the query with which Cub supplemented his father's observation.

"That, of course, we don't know," the latter replied. "They may have taken him over to the Canadian shore and released him for reasons of their own."

"Then it's up to us to find out," Cub inferred.

"Surely. We've had remarkable success thus far. It would be a pity for us to meet with failure. That would spoil our story."

"Story!" exclaimed Bud. "What story?"

"Our story—the one we've been enacting thus far. Look back over our experiences in the last two days and see if you can make anything but a very fascinating yarn out of them."

"It's a radio-college story, isn't it?" Hal suggested.

"Yes," Mr. Perry agreed; "that would be one good way to put it."

"If it didn't involve my cousin in a critical situation, I'd hope the story wouldn't end yet," said Hal. "I'd like to see it run thirty or forty chapters."

"How many chapters do you figure it would make thus far?" asked the director-general of the expedition with a look of keen interest.

"Oh, about ten or fifteen," Hal replied.

"Then, to suit your taste, it ought to be only about half finished."

"Yes, but for my cousin's sake, I wish it were finished right now and

Alvin were safe with us or at home."

"But wishes won't produce results nor cut off chapters," Cub philosophised.

"No, the denouement will work itself out along natural lines under natural laws," Mr. Perry predicted.

"I don't think this story is going to amount to anything as a yarn," Cub announced with a look of superior wisdom.

"Why not?" asked his father.

"Because there's no villain in it. I never did like a story with a tame ending, and the worst kind of a story on earth is one that starts with a thrill and ends with a nap in a sunparlor."

Laughter greeted this grotesque contrast.

"I don't think you need expect any such up-shot in this affair," Mr.

Perry advised.

"Do you expect a villain to show his hand?" Bud inquired.

"It seems to me that we have some villains in the plot already."

"Who are they?" asked Hal.

"How about those sophomores who kidnapped your cousin and marooned him here?"

"Oh, they're only play villains," Cub put in disdainfully.

"How do you know they wouldn't do something worse than haze freshmen?"

"I don't; but until they do they're just play villains, and that doesn't interest me."

"I see," Mr. Perry observed; "you want people to be either very good or very bad."

"No," Cub returned slowly. "I wouldn't put it that way; I don't want anybody to be bad at all; but the fact of the matter is there are lots of good people in the world and a good many bad."

"And to make a good story you think it is necessary to bring good people and bad people together, eh?"

"Well, that's what makes fireworks, isn't it?"

"Oh, ho, I get you now," said Mr. Perry. "You're fond of spectacular things."

"No, I wouldn't put it that way," Cub replied; "but I don't like to see anybody make a bluff at anything and not make good. Now, we've started out with a glorious bluff at some very clever rascality, and it looks as if it's going to prove to be just an ordinary hazing affair."

"It looks to me like a very extraordinary affair, whether it was hazing or not," returned his father.

"And you think we'll find a villain if we investigate it to the end?"

"Why, sure," Mr. Perry smiled. "I shouldn't be surprised if we'd find

Captain Kidd's treasure buried on this island."

"Now you're joking," Bud put in.

"What kind of mathematics would you use to locate that treasure?" Hal inquired with a kind of jovial challenge.

"Cube root," was the reply.

"That means dig at the roots of a four-cornered tree and you'll find a box of pieces of eight shaped like a gambler's dice," Cub inferred.

"That's pretty good imagination, and, I think ought to put us in a frame of mind well suited for further investigation," said Mr. Perry. "Now let's go to the spot where Hal found that diary of his cousin and see if we can't discover something more of significant interest."

CHAPTER XV

The Hook-Up on Shore

Arrived at the open area where Hal had found his cousin's "Crusoe diary", the three boys and Mr. Perry began a careful examination of the surroundings for further evidence that might throw light on the strange affair, which, for the time at least, appeared to defy the mystery scoffer's "mathematics".

First they scrutinized every foot of ground where the grass had been trampled so violently, it seemed, as to suggest a physical combat. But they were not sufficiently skilled in the arts and subtleties of the aborigines to work out the "code" of footprints and twists, tears, and breaks in the grass, twigs and foliage. So the result of the inspection of an apparently recent battle ground was nil.

"I believe we've exhausted every possibility of a clew to the mystery in this spot," declared Cub at the end of half an hour's search. "Let's not waste any more time here."

"What'll we do next, then?" asked Bud.

"Go fishin'" Cub replied.

"I think that's a good suggestion," said Mr. Perry. "We've concentrated our minds and efforts on this problem all day thus far, and a little relaxation probably will do us good."

"Where's the best place to fish?" Hal inquired.

"I think I know," Bud replied. "I found a place where we can climb down the bank to a dandy little beach while I was looking over my section of the island. A little spur of land runs out at that point, so as to form a small bay, and the water there is quiet and looks deep."

They returned to the camp and got their fishing tackle and soon were casting baited hooks into the bay. Bud's prediction as to the hopeful appearance of this place, from an angler's point of view, proved well founded. In less than an hour they caught more fish than they could eat at supper and breakfast.

After supper they formed a campfire circle in front of the tent—without a fire, however, for the normal heat of the atmosphere was all that comfort could demand—and held a further discussion of the situation and the problem with which they were confronted.

"I don't know, boys, but we ought to make a trip somewhere in the Catwhisker and get police help to solve this problem," Mr. Perry remarked with a reflection of years and judgment in his countenance. "Hal's cousin may be in serious trouble, for all we know, and it's our duty to enlist every agency at our command to aid him."

"But while we're gone something might develop here that would throw light on the mystery," said Bud. "Excuse me, Mr. Perry, for insisting on calling it a mystery. I can't think of it as anything else."

"Oh, goodness me!" returned the one thus addressed. "I'm afraid you boys failed to get what I was driving at. I didn't mean there was no such thing as mystery. That depends on your point of view. It is only people who are easily startled or confused by unusual things who are easily mystified. I don't mean to say that it would be impossible to mystify me under any circumstances. For instance, if the man in the moon should suddenly jump down on the earth and give me a brick of green cheese, and then jump back again before I could say 'thank you' I presume I'd be greatly mystified."

"Your illustration won't stand a test of reason, dad," Cub objected. "To test whether it is possible for you to be mystified you must offer a test that is possible."

"That's precisely why I offered that impossible illustration," Mr. Perry smiled. "I wanted to see if any of you boys would catch the inconsistency. You just call this affair a mystery as long as you think it is one, but after it is cleared up, I fancy you'll have difficulty in looking back and picturing it as a mystery in your minds. But I didn't intend to take us off our subject. I was going to answer Bud's argument that something of importance might develop while we were gone. Yes, that is true, but it wouldn't be necessary for all of us to go. Two of us might make the trip and the other two remain here."

"That's a good idea," declared Hal. "Suppose you and Cub go and leave Bud and me here to look after the camp and watch for developments?"

Mr. Perry did not reply at once. Something new seemed to have slipped into his mind and appeared to be giving him some concern.

"On second thought," he said after a few moments of silence; "I'm inclined to withdraw my suggestion."

"What's up now, dad?" Cub inquired.

"I was just recalling a portion of Hal's cousin's diary," his father replied. "According to that, it seems that rough characters visit this place sometimes."

"Oh, we're not afraid," Hal protested. "Besides, you could make the trip there and back in a few hours."

"Well, we'll think it over and decide in the morning what we'll do," said

Mr. Perry.

"Meanwhile, I tell you what we ought to do," Bud proposed. "It's an hour before dark and we'd have time to bring Hal's wireless outfit up here and hook it up before the sun sets."

"That's a peach of an idea," declared Cub, jumping to his feet in his eagerness. "I've got two hundred and fifty feet of extra wire and some insulators on the boat and we can put up an aerial here without taking down the one on the Catwhisker. Then we can shift the radio outfit back and forth to the island and to the boat as we please."

"Good!" exclaimed Hal. "I'm with you on that. Let's get busy and not waste a minute of daylight."

They worked rapidly, and as they were well supplied with material and tools the progress made by them measured up to expectations. They fashioned a two-wire antenna with the spreaders left on the island by Hal's cousin; connected a lead-in to this, and then Cub and Bud climbed the two trees and, with the aid of ropes tied around their waists and the guiding assistance of their companions below, drew the "ether-wave feeler" up to a lofty elevation and fastened it as nearly taut as they could stretch and hold it. In this work they took due consideration of the professional objection to tree entanglements in aerials so that the insulators were well beyond the reach of the longest limbs.

"It's a simple matter now to bring the outfit ashore and hook it up with the aerial," said Hal. "Let's do it."

Enthused by the novelty of their enterprise, they continued the work, even though dusk was rapidly gathering. Several electric-battery flash-lights were produced, so that the twilight did not seriously hinder them. By the time the stars had become a billion glittering gems in the sky, the hook-up had been completed with Hal's sending and receiving set on a table that had been transported from the yacht to a convenient position directly under the aerial and near the opening of the tent.

"Now, let's see what's going on in the air," said Cub. "Hal, you take the first whirl through the atmosphere."

Hal sat down by the table and put a pair of phones to his ears. Then he began to tune. First there came to him a discordant confusion of static and other noises, including an admixture of "ham impudence".

"W H Q's on," announced Hal presently, pushing over the horn switch, whereupon the clear tones of a quartet from the Rochester station was thrown with amplified resonance out upon the reamplifying atmosphere of a land-and-water wilderness.

They "sat through" the program with a degree of enjoyment never before experienced by them under a radio spell. They could almost imagine themselves on an enchanted isle with a band of fairy songsters teasing harmonious echoes out of their surroundings.

"My! I didn't suppose such weird beauty of sound could be produced under any possible conditions," exclaimed Mr. Perry at the close of the last number on the program.

"Now the air will be free for all for a short time," said Hal, putting on the phones and throwing back the horn switch, while the other boys also donned their phones. "I'm going to see if I can get any of those fellows we talked with on the way up here."

"Get that amateur with the radio compass who proved Mr. Perry's mathematical theory," suggested Bud.

"All right I remember his call and wave length; so here goes."

Hal tuned for several moments and sent the call of the Canadian amateur in question. Then suddenly he gave a little gasp of surprise. Only Mr. Perry felt a curiosity as to what it meant, for the other two boys knew as soon did the boy at the transmitting key. Someone was calling them and the call he gave as his own was the Canadian V A X. Then came the following message:

"Have you not given it up yet, boys? I did not mean to carry the joke so far. Better go back home."

Mr. Perry was waiting patiently for an explanation of the tense interest manifest in the attitudes of the three boys. Presently Cub gave it to him, thus:

"We're on the trail again, dad. This fellow we've got is posing as Hal's cousin and he's advising us to go back home."

CHAPTER XVI

Running Down a Radio Fake

"You say you are V A X?" dot-and-dashed Hal to the amateur who had thus represented himself.

"Yes," was the reply.

"What is your name?"

"Alvin Baker."

"Where do you live?"

"At Port Hope."

"Where are you now?"

"On the river with some friends."

"Have you any relatives in the United States?"

"Yes."

"Where do they live?"

"In New York."

"New York City?"

"No—State."

"What city?"

"I have forgotten."

"Is it Rochester?"

"I do not know."

"Is it Oswego?"

"I am not certain."

"Have you a cousin named Hal?"

"Yes."

"What is his last name?"

"Baker."

"Have you any relatives named Stone?"

"I think so."

"Is the name Hal Stone familiar to you?"

"Never met the gentleman."

"Then your name is not Alvin Baker?"

"Maybe you know my name better than I do."

"No, but I know just as well as you do that you are not Alvin Baker."

"How do you know that?"

"Because Alvin Baker is my cousin. I am Hal Stone, and I live in Oswego, New York."

"I do not believe you. You are an impostor."

"Let me tell you a secret. I have penetrated your plot. You are an enemy of my cousin. There was no wager between him and you, but you don't want us to find him. You had better keep out of the atmosphere or I will have you arrested on a charge of disorderly conduct in the air."

No answer.

"V A X, V A X, V A X," called Hal.

Still no reply.

"I cornered him, proved he was an impostor, and now he won't talk to me any more," said Hal, addressing his companions. Then he translated the code conversation, just completed, for the benefit of Mr. Perry.

"Well, that disposes of him for the time being, at least," was the latter's comment.

"But leaves a mystery as to his identity," put in Bud with a "mystery smile".

"No, I don't think there's any question as to his identity."

"Have you worked it out by mathematics, dad?" Cub inquired.

"Yes, by sines and cosines."

"What are sines and cosines?" asked Hal.

"You'll find out when you go to college and study trigonometry," Mr. Perry replied.

"Oh, I've seen those words," Cub answered, with some of his alleged characteristic "highbrow eagerness". "You spell sine, s-i-n-e, and cosine, c-o-s-i-n-e."

"Exactly," smiled Mr. Perry. "Those are terms used in higher mathematics. But, in order that you youthful minds may not work too hard over my trick, I'll admit that in my mind I spelled sine s-i-g-n, and cosine, c-o-s-i-g-n."

"No use to try to get ahead of my father," Cub declared, shaking his head. "He could prove that water runs uphill by mathematics. He means the signs and cosigns indicate that—. What do they indicate, dad? We got off the question just because you wanted to carry your point with a pun."

"I meant to say that this fellow whom you cornered and chased out of the air is one of the fellows who hazed Hal's cousin by marooning him on this island," Mr. Perry answered.

"Gee! that never occurred to me," exclaimed Cub, swinging his long arm with a snap of his finger like the crack of a whip. "I bet anything you're right."

"We get one step nearer every time we make a move," said Bud eagerly.

"Yes, but the question is, how many steps do we have to take before we settle this—this—mystery?" Cub demanded.

"Don't look ahead so far," Mr. Perry warned. "Here's a rule in such matters that applies to all men—and boys—of small or large capability. Be careful never to look ahead so far you can't see the step you are in the act of taking."

"All right," Cub assented. "What is the next step for us to take?"

"Find out who the fellows are that hazed Hal's cousin." Bud replied.

"Yes, that's a good suggestion, though it'll probably require several steps to gain that information. Still, you're not looking so far ahead, when you propose that move, as to be unable to see your first step."

"Why not try to get in touch with some amateur in Cousin Alvin's home town by wireless?" Hal suggested.

"That's the very thing I was in hope one of you would propose," Mr. Perry replied. "You boys haven't by any means exhausted the possibilities of your radio outfit."

"We have no Canadian call book," said Hal, "but perhaps I can induce one of the amateurs we've been talking with to look up the call of one or more amateurs in Port Hope and give them to me."

Without more ado, he swung the switch into sending position and began to call the amateur who had given them the information that had enabled them to locate Friday Island. Success rewarded his efforts almost immediately. The curiosity of the Rockport amateur, however, had to be satisfied before further service could be had from him. This Hal did with due patience and speed, reciting their experiences since their arrival at the island. Meanwhile the Canadian consulted his call book, and was ready with the desired information by the time his very excusable curiosity had been satisfied. He supplied Hal with two Port Hope calls, together with their wave lengths.

Then began the task of getting into communication with the Port Hope amateurs. Hal sent the call of each of them a score or more of times, but got no answer from either. At last, however, another Port Hope amateur, who chanced to be listening in, answered for them. He informed Hal that the sending outfit of one of these Port Hope boys was out of working order and the other amateur was out of town. Then the operator on Friday Island put the following questions to him:

"Do you know Alvin Baker?"

"Yes," was the reply.

"Is he at home?" Hal continued.

"I think not. He is at college."

"I am his cousin, Hal Stone, from Oswego, New York. I am with some friends on an island in the St. Lawrence River. I have learned that Alvin is in trouble. He was hazed by some sophomores, who left him alone on an island in the river. We found the island, but Alvin had been spirited away and is probably being held prisoner by them. This hazing gang seems to consist of some pretty rough characters. I want to get in touch with my uncle, Alvin's father."

"I will call your uncle on the telephone and tell him what you say," the

Port Hope amateur dot-and-dashed in reply.

"Ask him to come over to your house, and tell him I will explain everything to him through you, and then perhaps he can form a plan for his son's rescue."

These and subsequent proceedings, in furtherance of the plan outlined "over the wireless" by Hal, took considerable time, but at last the situation was made clear to Mr. Baker, who announced his intention to start on a search for his son at once. Meanwhile Bud and Cub listened-in eagerly and translated the code messages for Mr. Perry.

"I tell you what we'll do," the latter said after the communication of events had been completed for the benefit of Mr. Baker. "Tell him to take a train to some river port, the nearest possible to this island, and we'll meet him with the motor boat."

Hal did as requested, and presently Mr. Baker caused this message to be sent:

"I will meet you at Rockport about noon to-morrow."

"Step number one proved to be well worth while," observed Mr. Perry. "Now let's go to bed and in the morning we'll take step number two."

CHAPTER XVII

Bud's Discovery

Next morning the day's program was discussed at the breakfast table, the latter being a light collapsible affair carried as an item of equipment of the Catwhisker. Hal introduced the subject by saying:

"Mr. Perry, don't you think two of us ought to stay here while the other two of us make the trip to bring Uncle John over here?"

"What's the use?" Mr. Perry returned. "Nobody's going to run away with the island."

"No, but we've established a camp here, pitched a tent, and brought ashore a lot of camp material and supplies. If we all go we'll have to strike the tent and take all these things back on the boat."

"Well, I don't know that it makes any particular difference to me," the owner of the yacht replied. "It'll be broad daylight and we'll be gone only a few hours. It isn't at all likely that anything will happen during that time."

"I'll stay here with Hal, if he wants to stay," Bud volunteered.

"That would be about the only way to arrange it," said Mr. Perry. "I don't like to have any of you boys make the trip without my being along, and as Cub knows the engine of the Catwhisker better than any other member of our party, I think I'd better take him with me."

"That's the best arrangement," said Hal. "And while you're gone, Bud and

I'll play Robinson Crusoe and Friday."

"Who'll be Crusoe and who'll be Friday?" Cub inquired.

"Oh, we won't quarrel about that," Bud replied. "Hal may have his choice and I'll take what's left."

"This plan will simplify matters, to say the least," Mr. Perry announced.

"About all we'll have to do when we decide to start is start."

"You don't need to wash any dishes before you go," said Bud.

"Friday'll do that."

"There you go already," laughed Mr. Perry. "I predict a revolution on this island before we return."

"No, nothing of the kind," Bud returned. "I was assuming that the lot of

Friday would fall to me. In other words, I volunteer to wash the dishes."

"I think you'll both have to be Fridays," Cub advised. "The real Crusoe of this place has disappeared and we don't want anybody usurping his honors in his absence. It is our duty to find him, reinstate him here, and then rescue him."

"And make prisoners of the buccaneers who marooned him," suggested

Mr. Perry.

"Yes, and make them walk the plank," added Bud.

"We're not exactly right in calling Hal's cousin a Robinson Crusoe, are we?" asked Cub reflectively. "You know Crusoe wasn't marooned; he was shipwrecked on his island."

"Yes, but Crusoe was just a hero in fiction, you know," Mr. Perry replied. "Alexander Selkirk, the real Crusoe, was marooned on an island in the south Pacific."

"Too bad he didn't have a wireless outfit," said Hal.

"Well, boys, my portion of the breakfast is stowed away, and I must remind you that the moments are fleeting rapidly," announced the director of the expedition presently. "Cub, are you ready to start?"

"All ready," the latter replied, rising from his chair and turning the "finish" of a cup of coffee down his throat.

"I would suggest that you boys try to raise some amateur over in Rockport and probably you can stir up some local interest there in this affair," Mr. Perry suggested. "I'm always in favor of all the publicity that can be had in cases of rascality, and this looks to me like something more than a mere hazing."

"Why, dad, I haven't heard you say anything like that before," said Cub, with a curiously inquiring look at his father. "What do you mean by that?"

"I don't know," was the reply. "Maybe it's our remarks about Crusoe, buccaneers, marooning, and walking the plank that worked on my mind and set me to thinking about outlaws. I've just got a feeling that this affair isn't going to be explained along any play lines."

"But Hal's cousin didn't have any suspicion that it was anything more than a hazing affair, according to his diary," Cub reminded.

"I'm not so sure about that, either. You know he explained his distress messages by saying that he had been marooned by some river thieves or bandits."

"But he said in his diary he didn't want to tell the truth," said Hal.

"True, but he may have had a suspicion, nevertheless, that he felt was not tangible enough to incorporate in his diary. However, that will all be explained in due time, let us hope. Now, let's hurry. Good-bye, Hal, Bud. We'll be back as soon as possible."

A few minutes later that Catwhisker was backing out of the narrow harbor with Cub and his father aboard and Bud and Hal on shore watching their departure. Presently the yacht was out of sight from their hemmed-in position, the view being obstructed by trees and tall bushes on an intervening isle, which constituted a link of the insular chain that surrounded Friday Island.

"Now, let's wash the dishes," said Bud, turning back toward the camp.

"I thought Friday was going to do that work," Hal reminded with a broad grin on his face.

"Wasn't it ordered that both of us should be Fridays?" Bud demanded smartly.

"You win," laughed Hal. "But here's a better way to handle the subject in view of another duty before us. You know we're supposed to try to get in touch with somebody by radio at Rockport and we haven't much time to spare before the Catwhisker arrives there. You get busy on the job and I'll take care of the dishes."

"Not on your lightning switch," returned Bud emphatically. "I volunteered to be Friday, and I'm not going to slip out of my promise through your generosity. You get busy with the key and the phones and I'll get busy with the dishrag."

As no reasonable argument could be adduced to defeat this proposition, the two boys were soon busy as prescribed by the last speaker. Bud's task required only about fifteen minutes, and after it was finished he rejoined his companion at the radio table.

"Well, what luck?" he inquired.

"Nothing doing," Hal replied. "I've managed to get the calls and waves of two amateurs at Rockport, but neither of them answers."

"Keep it up anyway," Bud urged, "and I'll take a tackle and go over to the place where we took in our haul of fish yesterday, and see what I can do this morning. Call me if you get anything interesting."

Hal promised to do as requested and then Bud hurried away. The former continued his efforts unsuccessfully with the sending key for nearly half an hour, hearing no sound from his friend in the meantime. Then he was about to take the receivers from his ears and go in search of the fisher-boy to find out what success he had had, when the latter appeared on the scene with a look in his face that startled the youth at the radio table.

"What's the matter, Bud?" Hal inquired, as he literally tore the phones from his ears. "Has anything happened?"

"Not exactly," the other replied. "But I've made a discovery that may mean trouble for us. At least, we'll have to be on the lookout from now on."

"Why—what do you mean? Hurry up; don't keep me in suspense. What kind of discovery have you made?"

"I've discovered that we're not the only persons on this island," was

Bud's chilling response.

CHAPTER XVIII

Unwelcome Visitors

"Why, Bud, what do you mean?" Hal demanded, in astonishment. "Who else is on this island?"

"Some men. I don't know how many," Bud replied in cautious tone. "I heard them talking about us. But keep your voice low, for this island is small and they may hear you."

"I was going to remark that this is a small island to contain much of a hiding place for anybody."

"Yes, but it's wild with bushes. And these men are bad fellows, I could tell from the way they talked about us. They're as mad as hops 'cause we're here. They're studying how to get rid of us without making more trouble for themselves."

"That's funny," Hal remarked. "Why should they care if we're here? Do they claim they own this island?"

"I don't know whether they do or not. I didn't hear them say anything about that."

"Where are they now?"

"Over near our fishing place, if they haven't left. They were hidden in some bushes, and I might 'ave run right into them if it hadn't been for their voices. After I heard them I kept myself under cover and crept closer till I could get what they said."

"Were you listening to them all the time you were gone?"

"Just about."

"And didn't you find out anything more specific than what you've told me?"

"No, I don't think I did."

"Why did you leave them?"

"They seemed to 've talked the subject dry and turned to other matters, and I thought I'd better come and tell you about it."

"And they're there yet?"

"So far as I know."

"After they'd talked their subject dry, what did they find to discuss?" asked Hal.

"Something wet," Bud answered with a grin.

"I get you; you mean they had some moonshine with them."

"Or some Canadian whisky."

"Probably that. But this makes the situation look a little better for us. If they're just a bunch of fellows out for a liquor outing, maybe we don't need to be much concerned about them if we keep shy of them."

"I don't think that's all there is to it," Bud replied, with a note of warning in his voice. "I heard one of them say we were likely to make trouble for them and we ought to be chased away and scared so badly we'd never come around here again, and the others seemed to agree with him."

"That sounds like a mystery," said Hal.

"I don't believe Mr. Perry would talk mathematics to explain such conversation," Bud declared.

"If he did, he'd probably make another pun about sines and cosines. But, say, don't you think we'd better make further investigation?"

"I don't know what we could do unless we did some more eavesdropping, and that might cause them to get ugly if they caught us in the act," Bud reasoned.

"Yes," Hal agreed; "I suppose we'd better wait as quietly as we can till

Mr. Perry and Cub get back; then we can decide better what to do."

"I don't see that there's anything for us to do but get away from here as soon as possible," said Bud. "Mr. Perry won't want to get into trouble with four men."

"He'll probably have a talk with them to find out what's on their minds," was Hal's conclusion.

"And then get out rather than have a fight," Bud added.

"Oh, I hope there won't be anything as bad as that."

"Why not, if we insist on staying? If these fellows are the rough characters we suspect them of being, that's the very sort of thing they'd resort to, provided, of course, that they thought they could get the best of us."

"Here they come now!" suddenly gasped Hal, indicating, with his gaze, the direction from which "they" were approaching.

Bud turned quickly and saw four men emerge from the thicket some fifteen feet to the rear of the tent. They did not look like rowdies, for they were fairly well dressed, but there was nothing reassuring in the countenance of any of them. One was tall and angular, another was heavy and of medium height, another was very broad-shouldered and deep-chested and had long arms and short legs, a sort of powerful monstrosity, he seemed, and the fourth was fairly well proportioned, but small. There was not a reassuring cast of countenance among them.

"We'll just have to stand our ground and hear what they have to say," Hal whispered: "Maybe they'll be reasonable if we don't provoke them. Be careful and don't say anything sassy."

"I won't," was the other's reassurance.

The four men approached to a point a few feet from the radio table and halted, and the tall angular man, assuming the role of spokesman, demanded in deep tones:

"What're you kids doin' here?"

"We're just waiting for some of our friends to come back," Hal replied.

"Where'd your friends go?" continued the spokesman with a leer that caused the two boys to shrink back a step or two.

"They just took a trip in the motor boat," replied Hal cautiously.

"They'll be back soon."

"Oh, they will, eh," leered the man as if he penetrated the weakness of the warning in the boy's answer. "How many are they of your friends?"

"More than we are," replied Hal, having reference to physical size of Mr.

Perry and Cub.

"Oh, come now, kids, tell us the truth," ordered the leering spokesman, advancing a pace nearer. "Tell us how many went away in your boat and how soon they'll be back."

"There was a large man and a big boy," Bud interposed with more assurance that he felt.

Sly grins crept over the countenances of the four men.

"Oh," grunted the spokesman; "you hope by that kind o' talk to scare us away. Well, nothin' doing along that line. This here island belongs to us, and we don't allow no trespassin."

"Is the island for sale?" inquired Hal, who thought he saw an opening through which he might work up the interest of the three men without arousing their antagonism.

"Fer sale?" repeated the spokesman of the quartet, all four of whom seemed to exchange among themselves a round of sinister glances. "Well, I guess nit. They ain't enough money this side o' the United States treasury to buy this island from us."

"We might be able to scrape up a handsome sum, if necessary," Hal reasoned.

A suggestion of covetous greed shone in the eyes of all four men, but the spokesman belied his own looks by saying:

"Nothin' doing. We want you guys to git out o' here. This is our summer resort, eh, Spike"—turning to the long-armed, deep chested man.

"Spike" nodded grimly and replied:

"You bet it is, cap'n. We're gen'lemen of leisure an' don't care fer money. All we want is our own, and they's sure to be trouble if anybody tries to take it away from us."

"Well, we don't want anything that doesn't belong to us," was Bud's reassuring answer; "and if this island is yours, we surely don't want to stay here. But we thought that maybe you'd be glad to sell, for a member of our party said he'd like to buy all of the islands of this group if he could find the owner."

"Who is he?" asked the quartet's spokesman.

"His name is Perry and he lives at Oswego, New York," Bud replied.

"Well, you all go somewheres else to talk that matter over and then take it up with my real estate agent. Meanwhile I don't allow no trespassers on this ground."

"But we can't go until our friends come back with their boat," said Hal.

"They promised to return soon."

"Where did they go?"

"To the Canadian Coast."

"What fer?"

"To get another friend who will join us."

"Well, they'd better hurry up or they won't find you when they get back."

"What's that you got there?" asked the man who had been addressed as

"Spike", indicating the radio table and outfit thereon.

"That's a wireless outfit, you goof," replied the tall, angular spokesman.

"I tell you what we'll do," Hal announced, taking inspiration from the attention thus called to his radio apparatus. "We'll call our friends by wireless and have them return at once and take us away. How's that?"

"All right," was the assenting response. "Go ahead, but be careful, no tricks, or our revenge will be speedy, and that's no name fer it."

With this warning the four men walked away and Hall got busy with a diligence inspired by a sense of danger and, at the same time, a sense of the opportunity afforded by the possibilities of the world's latest great invention, radio.

CHAPTER XIX

"S O S" from Friday Island

Max Handy, the Canadian youth at Rockport, who gave the crew of the Catwhisker, by wireless, directions whereby the latter were able to locate "mathematically" the whereabouts of the "Canadian Crusoe's Friday Island" listened in much of the time thereafter, in the hope of being able to keep in touch with developments to the end of this interesting radio affair.

And this hope was realized in a degree that could hardly have been expected with moderation. But he was well equipped, and, being mechanically inclined, and industrious, he was able to get a maximum of results with his sending and receiving outfit.

He had traced the rescue yacht all the way from Oswego to Friday Island, and the last message he had picked up from the three young radio Americans was the one that completed the agreement under which the yacht was to proceed to Rockport next day and meet the father of the "missing Crusoe". Then he attempted to get in communication with the island operator, but Mr. Perry had just announced that the next number on the program would be "everybody to bed at once", and there was no more listening-in before the next morning.

Max stayed up late that night, with phones to his ears, eager to get another message from the island, and he was a very much disappointed enthusiast when at last he gave up his efforts, convinced that they were useless. He slept late next morning and consequently lost an opportunity to respond to Hal's first call to enlist the aid of the Rockport amateurs in the campaign to rescue the missing "Crusoe".

But at last he caught a message from the island, and the conversation, translated from code, that took place between him and Hal, following a few introductory inconsequentials, was as follows:

"I listened-in last night and heard your arrangements for today," the

Canadian dot-and-dashed. "When are you coming to Rockport?"

"Two of us are on the way," Hal replied. "They ought to be there by this time."

"Is there anything I can do to help you?"

"Yes. Can you go to the dock and ask them to hurry back? There are four ugly acting men here on the island, who have ordered us off. They threatened to make trouble for us if we do not go soon."

"Don't your friends know those men are there?"

"No; we discovered them after the boat left."

"All right, I will run down to the dock and tell them."

Max literally kept his promise relative to his manner of travel. He ran all the way to the dock, half a mile. The Catwhisker was there, tied fast with cables, but nobody was on board.

"They've gone to the depot," he concluded; then he turned his steps toward the railroad station.

He ran and walked alternately, with a dozen changes of speed, and arrived just as the train from the west was pulling in. He had no difficulty in identifying Mr. Perry and Cub when they introduced themselves to Mr. Baker, as the latter stepped from a coach, and a moment later he was addressing the owner of the Catwhisker thus:

"Is this Mr. Perry of Oswego, New York?"

The latter turned quickly and beheld a youth about the age of his own son, but of considerably shorter stature.

"It is," he replied somewhat apprehensively, in view of recent stirring events and the logical probability of more of the same sort.

"Well, I have something important to tell you," Max continued. "I'm the boy who gave you the radio compass information that made it possible for you to find Friday Island."

"Gee! I'm glad to meet you," exclaimed Cub, seizing the Canadian youth by the hand and forgetting, in his eagerness, the announcement from the "radio compass detective" that he had "something important" to communicate.

But the latter, although equally pleased to meet the young amateur from the States, was on his guard against a delay of this sort and soon broke through the effusion of cordiality with which Cub greeted him and continued his communication thus:

"I was just telegraphing with one of the boys on the island, and he told me to tell you to hurry back. There are four men on the island who ordered them away and threatened to make trouble for them if they didn't get away soon."

"What's that!" exclaimed Mr. Perry, seizing the youth by the arms. "You say you got that kind of message from those boys?"

"Sure I did," the boy replied; "and they want you to hurry back."

"What kind of men are they—rough characters, bad men?"

"That's what I understood him to mean."

"Come on, Mr. Baker, Bob; we must hustle along. Thank you, my boy; you'll hear from me again."

"I'll hurry back and tell the boys I found you and you're on your way," shouted Max as he ran down the street toward home.

Mr. Perry led the way toward the dock at a rapid pace. Presently they found themselves in front of a hardware store, and the owner of the Catwhisker stopped and said:

"I'm going in here a minute."

He entered, and Mr. Baker and Cub followed, wondering a little as to the motive of the boy's father. But they were not long left in doubt.

"Have you any fire-arms on sale here?" Mr. Perry asked, addressing the proprietor.

"Small or large?" the latter inquired.

"Small."

"Right this way."

He stepped behind a show case in which was a display of automatics and revolvers. Mr. Perry selected one of the former and a box of cartridges and took out his pocketbook to pay for them.

"I believe I'll take one, too," interposed Mr. Baker, also producing a purse.

The storekeeper looked somewhat curiously at the two men.

"I'm supposed to exercise care and judgment in selling these weapons," he remarked slowly.

"Of course, of course," returned Mr. Perry. "The situation is this: We belong to a yacht on the river and have run up against some bad characters. I am the owner of the yacht and have decided that we need protection."

"Sure, sure, that's perfectly satisfactory," said the hardware man. "You can buy out my whole arsenal on that explanation."

"We won't need it," Mr. Perry smiled. "These two guns are enough."

The purchase completed, the two men and the boy left the store and hastened on toward the municipal docks.

Meanwhile Max arrived at his home and went direct to his radio room. There the first thing he did was to don his phones, and the result was instantly startling.

He had left the instrument tuned to the Friday Island wave length and the aerial switch in receiving position.

"S O S, S O S, S O S," crashed into his ears in rapid, energetic, excited succession, it seemed to his susceptible imagination.

Quickly he threw over the switch, and called for an explanation. It came as follows:

"Those men have seized my friend, and now are coming after me. S O S, S

O—"

That was all—not another dot or dash. Desperately Max appealed for further details, but it was like calling for life in a cemetery. The ether was dead, so far as Friday Island was concerned.

CHAPTER XX

Four Prisoners

When the Catwhisker arrived at Friday Island again, the place appeared to be deserted.

The camp was as they had left it, except that the breakfast dishes were washed and put away. "Friday" had performed his duty, but both boys had disappeared, and there seemed to be only one explanation of their disappearance, namely, the premonition of danger at the hands of the four strange men that the Rockport amateur, Max, had received from the boys on the island. No damage had been done to the tent or any of the camp paraphernalia, even the radio outfit being exactly as it had been when they left it in charge of Hal and Bud a few hours previously.

"This is getting pretty serious," Mr. Perry said, after they had made an unsatisfactory review of the situation. "I confess I don't know what to make of it."

Cub felt an impulse to brand this new affair as the most puzzling mystery that had yet confronted them, but he checked the utterance wisely enough as entirely too facetious for the occasion.

"We've got to get the authorities busy on this case," Mr. Perry added after a few moments' hesitation. "We may be sure now that it's more than a hazing affair. There must be a retreat of some bad men around here somewhere."

"What authorities shall we ask to help us?" Cub inquired.

His father seemed about to answer, but he hesitated a moment or two, with a puzzled look, first at his son, then at Mr. Baker.

"That's so," he said presently. "Where are we—in Canada or the

United States?"

"I think we ought to apply for help in both New York and Ontario," said Mr. Baker, who was ordinarily a man of quiet demeanor, but now was worked up to a state of nervous worry over the fate of his son.

"It's going to take some time to make trips to both sides of the river and get the authorities of New York and Ontario busy," said Mr. Perry; "but I suppose that's the only thing to do, and every minute wasted is an opportunity lost. So let's go right away."

"Hold on, father," Cub interrupted; "you forget that we have a means of calling help right here."

"It won't do to depend on your radio messages" his father replied. "You know the experience Mr. Baker's son had trying to get help that way."

"Yes, but there were conditions that queered his calls," Cub replied.

"Just remember the results we got by calling our new friend, Max, at

Rockport, and what he did for us. Unless I'm badly mistaken, we can look

for more help from him."

"Yes, you're right, Bob," Mr. Perry admitted. "But I don't like the idea of staying here and depending on a few boys to take care of so big a proposition. We need to arouse the whole country around here, including all people along the shores, on the islands and those boating up and down the river."

"In other words, there must be some real broadcasting," Cub interpreted.

"You bet you, and more than any amateur radio station in the country can do. Now, we've wasted too much time already. Come on; we've got to get started without any more delay."

"But let me stay and see what I can do while you're gone," Cub pleaded. "I bet I can have a police boat headed this way before you reach the mainland."

"No, nothing doing," his father ruled unwaveringly. "You'd disappear just the way the other boys did. We can't afford to run any more such risks."

"I'd be safe enough if you let me have that automatic o' yours, dad,"

Cub argued,

"No, sir-ree; I'm not going to leave you here alone to fight any gun battle with a band of bandits."

But the boy was still undismayed by his father's resoluteness. He had one more proposal to offer, and he presented it thus:

"You don't need to leave me here alone, dad. Mr. Baker may stay; you can run the Catwhisker alone."

Both men had started toward the landing place, expecting the boy to follow, but they stopped suddenly and faced about on hearing this new proposition. Mr. Baker looked almost eagerly at Mr. Perry, it seemed, and, observing that the latter's unyielding attitude had softened somewhat, he said:

"That's agreeable to me if it is to you."

"Well," returned Mr. Perry with slow deliberation, "that sounds pretty good. If it suits you both, it suits me. I don't think you'll have to use the guns, even if any bad actors do happen around. If you show them, that'll probably be enough. Do you know how to handle an automatic, Bob?"

"Sure I do," the latter replied. "All you have to do is keep the nose pointed away from you and toward the target you want to hit. To shoot, you just keep pulling the trigger, and when it's empty you're safe from accident until you fill the chamber again."

"That's a simple statement of facts," Mr. Perry smiled; "but you left out the most important of all, and until you tell me what that is, I'm not going to let you have it."

"Oh, I know what it is; you've told it to me lots of times," Cub replied with eager alertness. "You know, dad, I always remembered what you told me, and I didn't forget that advice of yours about fire-arms. It is, 'always handle an unloaded gun as if you know it's loaded.' I promise you, dad, I'll not forget it this time."

"I guess it's safe to let you have it," said Mr. Perry, handing over the weapon. "All right, now that everything's settled, I'll be gone and you two see what you can do through the air."

That ended the discussion, and a few minutes later the owner of the Catwhisker was putting all the speed he could put into the power boat toward the Canadian shore, while Cub devoted all his energy and skill to the task of summoning as much aid as possible by wireless, Mr. Baker standing by and waiting eagerly for results.

And results were not long coming. The yacht was scarcely out of sight beyond the outer rim of islands, when Cub recognized the call of Max Handy, the Canadian amateur at Rockport. He acknowledged the call, and then telegraphed the following:

"I am the boy whom you met at the depot a few hours ago. When we got back, we found the two boys we left here were gone."

"I knew something had happened," Max replied. "After I left you I got their S O S. Then one of them telegraphed that some men had seized his friend and were coming after him. His last message was broken off in the midst of a new S O S. I couldn't get him again, I called up the police and they said they would see it got to the proper authorities for investigation."

Cub translated this message for the benefit of Mr. Baker and was about to continue the telegraphic conversation when four men, armed with clubs, and with anything but friendly demeanor, appeared on the scene. Mr. Baker saw them first and sounded the alarm.

"Here they come," he said in low tone, the accents of which caused Cub to start to his feet and reach for his father's pistol which he had laid on the radio table. "Be careful," the man continued. "Don't shoot unless I do. Maybe we can get some information from those fellows. Put your gun in your pocket and don't draw it unless they attack us or you see me draw mine."

The movement of Cub, transferring the automatic from the table to the right pocket of his coat, did not escape the notice of the visitors, who appeared to have come from the wooded depths of the island. But evidently their uncertain vision left their minds in a condition of doubt as to the significance of the act, for they continued to advance, however, with some appearance of caution.

"I'll go forward a few steps to meet them," said Mr. Baker, in a low voice to Cub. "You stay back here and be careful with your gun. Don't use it unless you see me use mine; then keep your head. I think we'll be able to handle this situation without any violence."

He advanced half a dozen paces, then stopped and addressed the unwelcome visitors, who were now distant from him only about fifteen feet.

"Halt where you are, gentlemen," he said. "We are armed, and any further advance on your part will be met with the use of our weapons."

The "gentlemen" stopped with due consideration for the warning, but with scowls that indicated the poor grace of their obedience. A description of them would mark them as the ones who are heretofore recorded as having made an unfriendly call on Hal and Bud at the island camp earlier in the day. The tall, angular man again was spokesman for them.

"What're you fellers doin' on our island?" he demanded, with a deepening of his scowl.

"I didn't know the island belonged to you," Mr. Baker returned quietly.

"You don't happen to carry a deed to it in your pocket, do you?"

"No, but it's ours, or it belongs to one of us," the angry spokesman replied. "And we don't intend to allow any trespassing."

"We have no desire to do any trespassing," was the response to this veiled threat. "But I want to answer you with a clear statement of our position. We are here with a purpose and we don't intend to be turned aside from that purpose. To get down to brass tacks, three boys, one of them my son, have disappeared under remarkable circumstances from this island, and the indications point directly toward you men as responsible for their disappearance. What your motive is I have no idea, but you may be sure that it will be fathomed, and now that we have you in our power, we don't intend to let you get away from us. We are armed with automatic pistols that shoot like machine guns and one move either toward or from us, contrary to order, will start them barking. Now, my instruction to you is that you drop those clubs and come forward, one at a time, and allow my companion to search you for weapons."

As he spoke, Mr. Baker drew his pistol from one of his trouser pockets, and Cub did likewise. Instantly the scowls disappeared from the faces of the four men and were succeeded by looks suggestive of panic.

"There's no need of any such action by you," said the leader of the invaders with plaintive whine. "We ain't done nothin' out o' the way. We did drive those kids off o' the island, but we didn't hurt 'em. They're all right, and we c'n take you to 'em any time you want to go."

"How could you drive them off of here when they had no boat to go in?"

Mr. Baker demanded.

"Oh, we took 'em in our boat and put 'em on another island. If you'll agree to go away from here we'll produce those boys and land you anywhere you want to go."

"Why is it you're so anxious to have us go?" demanded Mr. Baker. "Is there something going on here that you don't want the authorities to know anything about?"

This shot seemed to throw confusion into the ranks of the visitors, judging from the expressions of their countenances. But their spokesman attempted to brush the inference aside as of no consequence to them by answering:

"That's foolish. If you think there's anything bad going on here, just bring on the police and investigate; but we don't intend to have anybody on these islands who hasn't any right here."

"Very well, we'll make a test of the question of rights so there won't be any dispute about it hereafter," said Mr. Baker. "Robert, will you call your friend at Rockport and tell him to send some officers here for four prisoners, but keep your weather eye on these fellows meanwhile and your pistol beside you ready for instant use."

Cub did as directed and soon was dot-and-dashing a thrilling message to Max Handy, who had been waiting apprehensively all this time for an explanation of the island operator's protracted silence.

CHAPTER XXI

The Hostage

Meanwhile the four prisoners held a furtive conference among themselves, and after Cub had finished his telegraphic conversation with the Canadian amateur, the leader of the worthy quartet addressed Mr. Baker as follows:

"Looky here, Mister man, we've decided that we're not going to stay here any longer. You ain't got nothin' on us, and you haven't got any reason to hold us up with those guns. We haven't done nothin' criminal, and we don't intend to be held for crim'nals. We'll tell you where your kids are and ev'rything'll be all right if you keep off o' our islands. We own all these islands here, and we're not goin' to 'low no trespassin'."

"The main trouble with your proposition is that we have no way of knowing whether you're telling the truth," answered Mr. Baker. "Can you tell us where the boys are and then prove that they're there before we let you go?"

"We c'n tell you where they are and you must take our word fer it," was the fellow's reply. "They're over on the first island in that direction, pointing to the southwest. You can't miss it. It's an island about the same size as this one, all by itself. You'll find 'em there if somebody hasn't taken 'em off."

"No, that won't do," replied Mr. Baker. "We can't afford to let you go."

"All right, then, let me tell you something more," said the spokesman of the strange quartet, whose self-confidence and courage seemed to be on the increase. "Do you see that stake there?"—indicating the visible end of a piece of wood similar to a guy-rope stake, that had been driven into the ground at a point midway between the two hostile conferees.

"I see it very plainly," Mr. Baker replied.

"Do you know what it means?"

"I must confess my ignorance."

"Well, I have a surprise for you. There are other stakes driven about a hundred feet apart clear across this island east and west. That is the dividing line between the United States and Canada. You are a Canadian, ain't you?"

"I am."

"Well, that line there means that you are now in Canada and we are in the United States. If you come over here to take us you are invading the United States. If you shoot at us, you are shooting across the border line at citizens of the United States. I defy you to commit any such act."

Mr. Baker was "almost taken off his feet" by the shrewdness of this argument, and for several moments he was unable to make any intelligent reply. Cub also was nonplused at the "international situation". However, the ludicrous element of the affair did not escape them, and presently Mr. Baker was hurling the following heated rejoinder at the spokesman of the unfriendly four:

"Now, see here, my fine fellow, I'm not going to listen to this nonsense any longer. My son has been kidnapped by you scoundrels, and I am a desperate man right now. I am in a mood at this moment to snap my fingers at international lines, if what you say is the truth. I don't care to dispute your word on so flimsy a subject. But here is the only compromise I am willing to make with you. One of you has got to stay here a prisoner until those boys are returned to us. I'm in dead earnest, believe me. If you try to escape, I'll shoot, and if necessary, I'll shoot to kill. Now you come right over here into Canada as quick as ever you know how, for if you don't, in a very few seconds I'm going to begin to shoot. I'm a good shot and my bullets will hit your feet first. Your companions may go and as soon as they bring back those three missing boys you may go, too. Now, come along into Canada. Hurry up, I'm going to count ten, and if you're still over there in the United States contaminating the soil and atmosphere of Uncle Sam with your impudence after I've stopped counting, I'm going to begin to shoot. If I have to bring you over into Canada, you'll come on a stretcher—see? Now I'll begin to count—one, two, three, four, five, six, seven, eight—"

The brave spokesman of the unwelcome visitors collapsed at Number 8 and shuffled rapidly toward the counter with the automatic pistol. His three companions, inspired, no doubt, with an eagerness commensurate with his panic, broke into a run and soon disappeared in the thicket at the rear of the camp.

"You'd better call after your friends and remind them that it's up to them to bring those boys back or your fate hangs by a thread," Mr. Baker advised as he proceeded to examine the fellow's pockets for dangerous weapons.

But the prisoner was either too sullen or too much frightened to respond to any suggestion requiring the exercise of wits. He merely obeyed clear-cut orders and turned a deaf ear to all other utterances on the part of his captors.

"We'd better secure him so that there'll be no chance of his getting away," Cub suggested. "There are some pieces of guy-rope in the tent. I'll get them and we'll fix him in a condition of safety."

Accordingly he went into the tent and a moment later reappeared with two pieces of rope, the strands of which he unplaited and knotted together, end to end, and then tested the knots by straining them across his knee.

"Now, we're ready," he said, addressing the prisoner. "Turn around and put your hands together behind you. There, that's right. I'll try not to be too cruel, but I must tie this rope pretty tight. Holler if it tortures you, but I must be the judge as to whether you can stand it. There, you won't be able to do any mischief with your hands. Now, come on; well go into the tent and take care of your lower extremities, as you know we couldn't afford to let you walk away. We have to hold you for ransom, you know, and the ransom is three healthy, uninjured boys."

The prisoner obeyed without a word, and a few moments later he was tied on the ground in the tent with legs also securely bound.

"Now, I'll proceed to report developments to our radio friend at

Rockport," Cub announced as he and Mr. Baker came out in the open again.

With these words he sat down at the table, donned the phone headpiece and began to work the key. He had no difficulty in getting into communication with the Canadian amateur again, and gave him a detailed account of what had taken place since his last report of earlier developments.

"My father is on the way alone in the Catwhisker, bound for Rockport," the boy added after finishing his account of the dispute with the professed owners of the island. "Can you get word to him of what has happened? Tell him to come back with a few armed men as soon as possible."

"I will run down to the docks and meet him," returned Max. "Maybe I will come along."

That ended their code conversation for the time being, and Max started at a brisk pace for the municipal docks.

Meanwhile, Mr. Baker and Cub kept an alert watch over their prisoner and the camp in general to guard against a surprise, for they were not unmindful of the danger of an attempt on the part of the three departed visitors to overthrow the advantage the man and the boy had gained through the instrumentality of two dangerous weapons. But soon they found time dragging heavily on their hands, so that it is no wonder that before long they began to cast about them for something to do that would add to the small degree of hopefulness of their situation.

"Let's bring that fellow out here and see what we can get out of him,"

Cub proposed at last. "Maybe we can induce him to tell us something,"

"All right," Mr. Baker replied; "but we must not forget to keep a sharp lookout while we're quizzing him."

"You go in and bring him out, and I'll keep watch to prevent a surprise,"

Cub proposed.

This being agreeable to Mr. Baker, the plan was soon put into effect. The rope strands around the prisoner's ankles were removed and he was led out into the open. True to his resolve not to be caught napping, Cub now kept on the move and on the alert, describing a small circle around the position of the two men who were seated on camp chairs about twenty feet from the tent.

"I've brought you out here for a sociable chat," Mr. Baker explained, while Cub gave close attention in order that he might not lose a word. "I hope you'll be as sociable as I shall try to be, for if you're not, I shall have to take you back into the tent and shackle your feet again."

The fellow did not reply, although his silence could hardly be attributed to a spirit of sullenness.

"Maybe you'll tell me a little more than you were willing to tell me in the presence of your friends," Mr. Baker continued. "I'd like to know something about the business and associations of you and your friends, so that we may know how to treat your demands. Now, rest assured that none of us has any desire to do any illegal trespassing, and as soon as you've proved to us that you own this island and that we are unwelcome on these premises, we'll get off and beg your pardon for our intrusion. But you don't seem to have established any camp here and you don't seem to be able to produce as much evidence of ownership as we can."

Mr. Baker now waited a few moments for a response to his introductory statement, but none came. The fellow seemed to be almost embarrassed by the straightforward and well connected ideas of the man who addressed him.

"Well, let's see," Mr. Baker continued. "How can I present the matter so as to start you out right? Perhaps you will be willing to tell me who you are and what your business is. But first. I'll be fair and introduce myself. My Name is James C. Baker. I live in Port Hope, and my business is that of hay, grain and feed merchant. Now, will you tell me your name? One of your friends called you Captain. Do you run a boat on the river?"

Whether the fellow was about to reply or would continue in stubborn silence may not be known, for the thus-far-one-sided conversation was suddenly interrupted by a shout of eager joy from the pacing boy sentinel.

"Oh, there they come, there they come," the latter shouted. "There are

Hal and Bud."

Sure enough, two boys had just emerged from the narrow belt of bushes between the camp area and the only practical landing place of the island.

CHAPTER XXII

The "Crusoe Mystery" Deepens

"Now, where have you boys been? Did those men take you away? Where did they take you? Did you escape? How did you escape?"

This rapid-fire succession of questions was hurled by Cub at Hal and Bud as they approached the place where Mr. Baker was quizzing his prisoner under the protection of the boy sentinel against a surprise attack from the prisoner's friends. Some of these questions were encouraged by nods and smiles of assent to preceding interrogatories.

"Yes, yes, but one question at a time," Hal replied. "You're on the right track, Cub, but that isn't the way to get our story out of us. I see you have one of the rascals a prisoner. Keep him. He's the worst of the bunch."

The "rascal" winced at the characterization.

"Who are they, anyway," asked Cub. "What are they doing here? Do they own this island?"

"Now, you've added three more questions," Hal remarked with a smile, for he was much pleased at the opportunity to tease the tall and usually super-wise youth in something of the latter's characteristic manner. "We can't answer all your questions, Cub, but we know there's a mystery about this fellow and his friends, and I suppose we'll have to wait for your father's mathematics to solve it."

"Was it those four men who made prisoners of you?" inquired Cub, who, in his eagerness to get some definite information, resolved to ask one question at a time and pursue his inquiry in an orderly manner.

"Yes," Hal replied.

"They grabbed me first while I was down at the landing," put in Bud, who was almost as impatient to tell the story as Cub was to hear it. "I went down there when I saw a rowboat pulling up and didn't recognize the men in it until they came ashore. I thought they were still on the island, for when they left us a few hours before, they didn't go toward the landing, and we didn't see them go toward it since then. I hollered when they grabbed me, and Hal came rushing to see what was the matter."

"Yes, and then I ran back to the radio table and telegraphed to Max Handy at Rockport," added Hal, taking up the narrative at this point and indicating a disposition to volunteer details more readily. "While I was still in the act of sending, two of the them appeared and seized me. They took me into their rowboat with Bud at the landing and rowed to a yacht almost a duplicate of Mr. Perry's. We were confined in the cabin until after dark and then put ashore on an island half a mile from here. That was the last we saw of them."

"But how did you get away?" asked Cub.

"We flagged a motor boat just a little while ago. There were two men and two boys in it. We told them our story and they volunteered to bring us back here and see if you had returned. Hello, Uncle James," addressing Mr. Baker and seizing the latter by the hand. "I didn't recognize you at first, though I knew you were coming."

"Where is Alvin?" asked Mr. Baker anxiously. "Didn't you see him on the island over there?"

"No," Hal replied with a look and tone of surprise. "That is another desert island—not a person there."

"What does that mean?" demanded Mr. Baker, turning to the prisoner. "You told us all three of the boys that you took away from here were together on that island over there."

"I didn't mean that," the fellow snarled, with something of a look of confusion, however.

"Well, what did you mean?"

"I meant they were on two islands not far apart; the other fellow is on the island a little further on."

"Is that motor boat that brought you here down at the landing yet?" Mr. Baker inquired.

"Yes," Bud replied.

"I wonder if we couldn't induce them to make a run over to the island where this fellow says he left my son and bring him here."

"I think they'd be glad to do it," Bud replied. "They seemed to be very much interested in this affair and offered to do anything they could to help us."

"All right; suppose you go down there and tell them the situation. I suppose we could wait till Mr. Perry gets back, but I can't stand any delay that isn't absolutely necessary."

"Why, where has your father gone, Cub?" asked Hal.

"He started out to get police help," answered the boy addressed. "His first call was to be at Rockport, but no doubt he'll come right back here when he gets the message I sent for him. I telegraphed to our wireless friend, Max Handy, and asked him to go down to the docks and tell father what happened since he left. He's on the way now; maybe he's talking to father this minute."

"What was it that happened?" Bud inquired.

Cub gave a description of the visit of the four "owners" of Friday Island and the dispute that resulted in making a prisoner of one of them and sending the other three away on a mission of restitution.

"I thought when I just saw you come up from the landing that they had released you according to agreement," he added; "but on second thought, I decided they couldn't have had time to do that; besides, when they left us they went in the other direction."

"No, they didn't have anything to do with it," Hal assured his friend.

"You'd better tell the truth about where my son is," warned Mr. Baker, addressing the prisoner. "I won't stand any more trifling from you."

"He's there unless somebody took him off the island, same as these boys were taken off the island we put them on," declared "the captain" in sullen tone and manner.

"Well, it'll be an unhappy circumstance for you if we don't find any evidence of their having been there," Mr. Baker remarked.

"I think we'd better take him along with us," said Hal. "Then there'll be no doubt about our going to the right island. Come on, Bud; let's go down to the boat and tell Mr. Leland and Mr. White what we want to do."

Hal and Bud were soon out of sight on their way to perform the mission they had imposed on themselves, and a few minutes later they returned with one of the motor-boatmen, a clean-cut athletic man of middle age, wearing a tan Palm Beach suit. Hal introduced him as Mr. White.

"The boys have told us all about your trouble," he said, addressing Mr. Baker; "and we'd like to do all we can to help you out. They tell me that your son is believed to be on an island about a mile from here, and that this prisoner of yours knows exactly where that island is. Well take him along with us and make him make good."

"I'm very much obliged to you," said Mr. Baker warmly. "I've promised this fellow that if he returns my son to me, I'll let him go, so the instant you find my son you may turn him loose."

"I don't believe he ought to be turned loose," declared Mr. White energetically. "I believe he ought to be made to pay the penalty of his crime—kidnapping. However, we'll do as you say. Come along, my fine fellow," he added, taking the prisoner by the arm. "We'll keep those hands of yours securely tied behind your back, so you can't get into mischief."

With these words, he led "the captain" toward the landing, followed by

Hal and Bud.

Half an hour later they returned, with the prisoner, his hands still shackled with the rope strands. They had been unable to find Mr. Baker's son on the island where the prisoner said he and his companions had left him.

Meanwhile Mr. Perry had returned in the Catwhisker to Friday Island. He was accompanied by Max Handy and a Canadian government officer.

CHAPTER XXIII

"Sweating" the Prisoner

It was now supper time, but nobody except the Canadian officer was hungry enough to think of eating. The latter, being a disinterested party, save as one commissioned with the duty of enforcing the law, had not diverted to a subject of absorbing interest the energies that ordinarily create a human appetite, hence he was normally hungry. Moreover, he was a man of good physical proportions and organic development, and consequently hunger with him meant a good plateful, or dissatisfaction.

This officer, who was introduced by Mr. Perry as Mr. Harrison Buckley, seemed to take no interest in his mission until he saw the evening meal in course of preparation in real kitchen-like manner; then he took the prisoner in charge and proceeded to "sweat" him in the approved style of a police captain's private office. The prisoner squirmed about for a time, successfully evading the inquisitorial probe aimed at him, but at last he "confessed" as to his name and address. He said that his name was Grant Howard and that his residence was at Gananoque, Ontario. Then a call to supper was issued and the composite aggregation of humans gathered around the table, which was never intended to accommodate quite so many guests.

However, with the exercise of due ingenuity, the supper was properly disposed of with the unexpected discovery of more appetite than was originally expected. Max Handy proved to be a healthy eater and the savory smell of juicy broiled steak from the Catwhisker's refrigerator, loosened even the nervous tension of Mr. Baker's worry over the fate of his son, so that he was able to do fair justice to the cooking of Cub, Hal, and Bud, who had full and joint charge of the preparation of the gastronomic spread.

After the meal the four boys cleared the table and washed and wiped the dishes, while the three men joined forces in the continued "sweating" of the prisoner. The latter adhered stubbornly to his earlier "confession" as to what he and his three companions had done with Mr. Baker's son, but failed to make a satisfactory statement as to his own business and the use to which he and his friends had put "their island possession". To the question as to the character of his business, he replied, after some hesitation:

"I work in a store."

"What kind of store?" asked Mr. Buckley.

"A grocery store."

"What do you do there?"

"I clerk."

"What was the price of butter the last day you worked?" asked the inquisitor so quickly and sharply that the victim of the thrust actually turned pale, in spite of a strong front of bravado. But he made a brave enough effort to get over the hurdle.

"Twenty-nine cents."

"A pound?" asked Mr. Buckley.

"Yes," replied the prisoner.

"What did you sell butter at a loss for?" the inquisitor demanded. "It hasn't been down that low anywhere that I know of since the war."

"I meant butterine," "corrected" the "sweat subject" hurriedly.

"Well, you've hit it about right, by accident, of course. Now, let's see if you know anything more about grocery business. What did you sell eggs and potatoes for the last day you worked?"

"I didn't sell any."

"All you sold was butter?"

"Yes."

"You mean butterine, don't you?"

"No, I sold butter and butterine and a few other things."

"And buttermilk and cheese," the officer amended.

No answer.

"How much did you charge for butter?"

"Fifty cents a pound," the prisoner replied, desperately or doggedly, it was difficult to determine which.

"Do you know that butter is selling now for thirty-nine or forty cents a pound?"

"Then it's come down."

"No, it hasn't. It's been around forty cents a pound for several months."

The prisoner fixed his eyes on the ground and said nothing.

"The trouble is, you haven't done your wife's grocery shopping, or you could tell a more plausible string of lies," Mr. Buckley commented. "Now, let me tell you this: It's been a long time since you saw the inside of a grocery store."

"If you don't want to believe me, it's up to you," snarled the prisoner.

"Now, Mr. Howard," the inquisitor continued, "your friends, I am told, addressed you as Captain. Why was that?"

This query stimulated a little brilliance in the fellow.

"I run a grocery boat on the river," he said. "I don't do much clerking, but supply groceries to several stores from a wholesale house."

"So that is your explanation for not being very familiar with retail prices, is it?" Mr. Buckley inferred.

"Yes."

"Well," the Government "sweater" went on, "your story doesn't hang together very well."

"You don't want it to hang together," the prisoner snapped. "You're here to make me out a liar. You don't want the truth. You haven't got no right to keep me here."

"He claimed the rights of a citizen of the United States and defied us to interfere with him," interposed Mr. Baker, who, together with Mr. Perry, had been listening eagerly to this quizzing process.

"How's that?" Mr. Buckley demanded.

"Why, Mr. Perry's son and I pulled guns on him and his three companions, when they threatened us with clubs, and this fellow pointed out what he said was the international boundary line between them and us and defied us to cross over and capture them. I made my bull-dog look at him squarely in the eye and hypnotized him over onto this side of the boundary line between the United States and Canada and made a prisoner of him."

"Where is that international boundary line?" Mr. Buckley asked.

"Right here," Mr. Baker replied, rising from his camp chair and walking about fifteen feet to the stake that the prisoner had designated as indicating the line beyond which any hostile advance must be regarded as a foreign invasion.

"Who put that stake there?" he inquired, shifting his penetrating glance from one to another of the three men before him.

"I don't know," replied Mr. Perry and Mr. Baker almost in one breath.

The prisoner said nothing, and Mr. Baker spoke for him as follows:

"If this fellow would answer, I presume the only statement he could make is that it was put there by surveyors of the Canadian and United States Governments."

"Humph! Funny surveyor's stake, isn't it?" grunted the Canadian officer, "Methinks we shan't go much farther to prove this fellow a fabricator of fairy tales. So that's the international boundary line, is it?" he asked, eyeing the prisoner keenly.

"I was told it was; that's all I know about it," the latter replied sullenly.

"Well that was a lucky reply if you intend to persist in your policy of evasion," Mr. Buckley declared. "I was about to denounce you as an illustrious liar. The boundary line between the United States and Canada along here, my dear sir, doesn't cut islands in two. If you will examine a map or chart of the Lake of the Thousand Islands, you will see that the boundary line winds like a snake, dodging the islands through its entire course in this part of the St. Lawrence river."

"It was foolish of me to swallow such a yarn as that," said Mr. Baker. "But I called his bluff good and strong. However, I'm much relieved to discover that my credulity was imposed upon; otherwise I might be accused of trying to drag the United States and Canada into war."

All of his auditors, except the prisoner, smiled at this remark. The boys, who had just finished washing the dishes, joined the inquisition group in time to hear Mr. Buckley's last statement and Mr. Baker's "confession of folly."

"I think we have got as much out of this man as we may hope to get at the present time," the officer announced a moment later. "I think I had better take him back with me and you had better come along, Mr. Baker, and swear out a warrant charging him with kidnapping."

"That's exactly what I'm going to do if my son is not returned to me to-night or early in the morning," answered the man thus addressed. "I suppose you have no objection to remaining here over night."

"Oh, no; it'll be easier to take care of the prisoner here over night than to work overtime, going back at night, and jail him. But we'll have to keep careful watch over him to-night and see that he doesn't escape."

"Maybe we'd better lock him up in one of the staterooms of the yacht,"

Mr. Perry suggested.

"Yes, and keep a good watch over him all night," Cub put in. "We want to make sure those three friends of his don't come back after dark and let 'im out"

"I'll watch with Mr. Buckley," Mr. Baker volunteered. "We're both armed and I don't think there's any chance of our being taken by surprise."

"We'll watch in two-hour shifts," Mr. Buckley proposed. "In that way we'll keep fresh and on the alert, so that there'll be less danger of being taken by surprise."

"Very well, that's agreed upon, if it's satisfactory to Mr. Perry," the officer announced.

Further attempts to get information out of the prisoner, bearing on the whereabouts of the place of concealment of Mr. Baker's son, were unavailing, and at last they separated into two parties for the night, Mr. Buckley and Mr. Baker taking charge of the prisoner on board the Catwhisker and Mr. Perry and the boys distributing the sleeping quarters among themselves in the camp.

But before the latter retired a new radio thrill was added to their adventures.

CHAPTER XXIV

"Something Happens"

"Something's going to happen to-night," Bud remarked to his three boy friends when the four found themselves alone after the departure of the prisoner under guard. Mr. Perry had accompanied the officer and Mr. Baker to the yacht to aid them in arranging comfortable quarters for the night.

"What makes you think that?" Cub inquired, while he and Hal and Max all gathered around the speaker, whose remark afforded stimulus in harmony with the weird twilight shadows around them.

"I bet I said only what you fellows were all thinking about when I spoke," Bud ventured by way of indirect reply.

"I felt it in my bones," Hal declared. "Bud didn't have any more reason to think something is going to happen to-night than all of us have. If something surprising doesn't happen, I shall be— "

" —surprised," finished Max, whereupon there was a chorus of laughter.

"Whatever happens, or doesn't happen, Hal is going to be surprised," Cub concluded facetiously.

"I think we all will be surprised," said Bud.

"Surprise party," shouted Hal.

"Bum surprise party without any girls," Cub added.

"Well, anyway, I think we ought to keep watch here to guard against the kind of surprise party we wouldn't like," Bud declared.

"I agree with you there, old boy," Cub put in quickly. "Whether or not anything happens, it would be jolly to have watches and relieve one another the way they used to do out west among the Indians and outlaws and road agents."

"I bet they do it yet in some places out there," said Max.

"Course they do," Cub concurred. "You can't tell me that the day of outlaws is gone. Think of the automobile bandits we have now-a-days. They'll be raiding with airplanes next."

"No, I don't believe that," Hal objected. "They couldn't use an airplane to any advantage. We won't have any more stage coach robbers or pirates on the high seas, and I don't think there's any chance of much of that sort of thing in the air, but there's a good chance for some bad doings in the air in another way."

"How's that?" asked Max.

"We've all had some experience with it, and you ought to know what I mean."

"Oh, I know," declared Bud. "You mean radio."

"Sure," replied Hal. "There are going to be a lot of con men at work in the air or some way in connection with radio; you see if there are not."

"They've been at work already," said Cub. "There's been a good deal in the papers about the games they work. But I'd like to know the truth about the fellow who tried to keep us from coming on this trip to find Mr. Baker's son."

"I bet he's somethin' more than a college sophomore," said Bud. "I wouldn't be surprised if he's connected in some way with the fellows who kidnapped our Thousand Island Crusoe."

"A big radio plot, eh?" Hal inferred.

"Maybe," Bud replied.

"What for? What could they be up to? Pretty far fetched isn't it?"

"Yes, maybe; but, you know, it's our business to think up every possible solution and then find out which one fits the facts."

"All right, Mr. Sherlock Holmes, but where's the sense in figuring this as a big radio plot unless we can see a sensible answer to it?" Hal demanded.

"Yes, Bud, it's pretty far fetched," ruled the dominating Cub. "You'll have to think up an answer to your conundrum before we can consider it. Why should a college freshman be hazed in the manner that Mr. Baker's son was hazed just so that some men, confederates of the hazers, could kidnap him? And then why should one of the hazers work the kind of game that that mysterious fellow worked to checkmate us in this rescue trip of ours if the purpose was just to kidnap Mr. Baker's son, after all? The sophomores had to kidnap him in the first place. Why go through all that Robinson Crusoe nonsense if the end was to be just a plain kidnapping?"

"Then you think there's no connection between the hazing and the kidnapping," said Bud.

"I don't see how there can be. There's nothing showed up yet that makes it look reasonable."

As Cub was making his last statement Mr. Perry returned to the camp. The speculative subject of discussion was then dropped for others more immediately practical.

"What did you do with the prisoner?" Hal inquired. "Did you lock 'im up in a stateroom?"

"That's what we did, and I don't believe there's much chance of his getting away with an armed guard constantly near his door," Mr. Perry replied.

"Are his hands and feet tied?" asked Cub,

"No, we decided that wasn't necessary. There's no way he could open the door without making a noise; so we thought we'd let him rest easy, and perhaps he'd be in a better humor in the morning and more willing to talk."

"We've been talking the matter over and we're all afraid something's going to happen to-night," said Hal.

"What do you think is going to happen?" asked Mr. Perry.

"We haven't any idea."

"Some more mystery, eh?" smiled the leader of the expedition. "Well, that isn't at all surprising, in view of the gloominess of our surroundings. Suppose we have a light on the subject. Cub, bring out the flash-lights."

The latter went into the tent and soon reappeared with four dry-battery lights. These he laid on the table in fan-like arrangement, so that they threw a flood of light in all directions.

"I don't feel like going to bed yet," said Cub. "Let's stay up a while and—"

"—listen-in," finished Hal.

"Yes, let's do," exclaimed Bud eagerly.

"I wasn't thinking of that," Cub admitted; "but it's better than what I had in mind. All right, Hal, tune 'er up. This is a peach of a night for long distance receiving."

Hal needed no second bidding and soon he was busy with coil and detector. Cub's "weather report" proved to be accurate, for in a few moments he announced:

"Here's Schenectady, New York, with some opera."

Over went the switch and with the move came a hornful of vocal resonance. They listened eagerly to the end of the program and then Hal began to tune about for "something else doing" in the ether. Presently he "straightened up" in an attitude of close attention, and his radio friends all realized that he had found something of more than ordinary interest.

"Here's a Watertown newspaper looking for information about us," he announced excitedly after a few moments of tense listening.

The other boys sprang forward with exclamations of wonder, Bud and Cub donning the other two phone head-pieces.

"Shall I give him the information?" Hal asked a few moments later, turning to Mr. Perry.

"Whom is he talking to?" the latter inquired.

"Some Canadian amateur who's been listening in to us a good deal of the time."

"I don't see why you shouldn't tell him everything, Mr. Perry. He's a reporter, isn't he?"

"Yes, I think he has his own private set and he's looking for a big scoop."

"Give it to him, by all means," Mr. Perry directed heartily. "Now the whole country will be aroused over this affair."

Hal managed to attract the attention of the reporter, although he did not know his call, and pretty soon the ether was alive with a torrent of thrills for the ambitious representative of the Fourth Estate. For half an hour the "radio interview" continued, during which many names and addresses were given and dramatic details were recited in the most approved manner of exciting spontaneity. At last, however, the close came with an announcement from the reporter that he was going to get a motor boat, make a dash to Friday Island, and "scoop the world". Hal gave him a careful description of the location of the island and assured the reporter that they probably would remain there a day or two longer.

"Now, we'd all better go to bed," Mr. Perry announced after Hal had tapped goodnight to the Watertown scribe.

"We ought to arrange some watches first," Bud urged, unforgetful of his prediction that something was going to happen before morning.

"Why do you think something more is going to happen?" inquired Hal. "You're a good forecaster, Bud, for your prediction has been fulfilled already. Something did happen when I caught that reporter and gave him our story."

"I'll say so," Cub "slanged" wisely. "We'll all have to take our hats off to you, tee-hee."

"Hal hasn't tee-heed for twenty-four hours in my hearing," Mr. Perry said reprovingly.

"That's right, Cub," declared Bud. "A little while ago I heard him laugh right down deep from his lungs."

"Out-door exercise is working wonders for him," Cub opined with deductive superiority.

"Well, anyway," said Mr. Perry; "I agree with Bud that we ought to have some watches to-night. I believe in taking warning from Bud's prediction. There are five of us. Who wants the first watch?"

Nobody answered.

"I'll take the watch beginning about 1:30 o'clock," said Bud. "If anything happens, it'll be between then and 2:30."

"Brave boy!" commented Cub solemnly. "I'll take next-best place, immediately following your watch."

"Give me the one just before Bud's," said Hal. "There may be something doing between now and then you know. If anybody invades the camp at 1:30 o'clock sharp, I'll call Bud and go to bed and let him repel the invaders."

"What a methodical bunch of boys!" Mr. Perry exclaimed.

"Due to the mathematical training we've had under you, dad," Cub explained.

"I'll take the first watch, if it suits everybody," Max announced.

"Say, father, you ought to let us have your automatic while we're on watch," Cub suggested.

"Nothing doing," replied the cautious adult, shaking his head vigorously. "I'd rather run the risk of being wiped out by a band of bandits than to run the risk of your shooting one of us if we should happen to walk in our sleep. If any of you boys see or hear anything suspicious, just call me, and I'll do the shooting, if any is to be done. You may arm yourselves with some good stout clubs if you wish to, however."

And so it was thus arranged, and while Max took his post on a camp chair in front of the tent, the other four sought rest on their cots under the canvas shelter.

CHAPTER XXV

Bud Shoots

For nearly half an hour Bud had kept his eyes fixed almost continuously on a certain spot in the dark shadow at the edge of the thicket directly south of the tent, which faced west. His attention had been drawn to this spot thirty or forty times after he relieved Max at 1:30 o'clock, and the cause of his interest was a slight movement in the shadow, suggesting a shifting of position by an animal of considerable size.

The moon was up, but not high enough to shed much light in the open area in which the tent was pitched. The sky was clear, and because of the deep shadows in which this spot was merged, the heavens, to Bud's eyes, were studded with myriads of gem-like brilliants.

In the dim light thus afforded, the boy sentinel was able to make out what appeared to be portions of the form of a man partly hidden in the bushes, which grew at heights varying from three feet to six or seven feet from the ground. Meanwhile he congratulated himself repeatedly for a bit of very ordinary ingenuity he had resorted to in order to prepare himself for any emergency of more or less menacing outlook.

Soon after Mr. Perry announced his intention not to allow any of the boys to have possession of his pistol while on guard, Bud's mind became busy on plans for the contrivance of a substitute. In accord with Mr. Perry's concession, each of the boys cut for himself a stout stick to be used as a weapon of defense if necessary, and to supplement this Bud decided first to gather a few dozen stones about the size of a hen's egg in order that he might exercise his skill at throwing if any suspicious looking objects should appear to his view.

Then he happened to remember that he had a large rubber band in a small and little-used pocket of his coat. He had put it there for no particular reason, perhaps merely to save it. He had found it about three weeks before and the unusual size and strength of elasticity of the band was enough to interest any boy in the habit of seeing the adventurous possibilities of little things.

With the aid of his searchlight, Bud found a small forked limb in a tree at the edge of the open area, immediately after he took charge of the guard post, and cut it off. Then he returned to his seat near the tent and began to whittle. The purpose of this whittling must soon have been evident to an observer, for he held the object up frequently and viewed it, with the calculating eye of a "dead shot," until at last he was satisfied with the length and "grip" of the handle and the symmetry and trim of the prongs of a fork.

Bud was always very methodical in his youthful mechanics. Everything he made must be "just so," hence the results were usually effective, as well as artistic to a degree. In this instance, even the notches that he cut around the extreme ends of the prongs were neatly grooved, in spite of the limitation of the light in which he worked. The only regret he had was the fact that he possessed no good strong cord, about the size of fishline, with which to attach two separate sections of the rubber band to the prongs at the grooves. As substitute for such cord he had provided himself with some strands of the rope with which the hands of their prisoner, "Captain" Howard, had been tied. After all the other details of his mechanical labor had been completed, he took from one of his pockets an old and inexpensive pouch-like pocketbook, emptied the contents into a trouser pocket and proceeded to cut out a section of the pouch to a size and shape suited to his needs. The rubber band he had cut into two equal lengths and in the leather section from his pocketbook he cut two small holes near opposite edges.

The assembling of the parts of his contrivance was now speedily accomplished, resulting in a very neat hand-catapult of a kind with which every boy is familiar. After testing the strength of the connections by stretching the rubbers several times to thrice their ordinary length, Bud looked about him and soon gathered a supply of small stones suitable for missiles.

He was thus engaged when he first observed a movement in the shadow of the thicket to the south of his position. Then, indeed, he congratulated himself on the preparation he had just made to defend himself and his companions against stealthy and hostile movements on the part of the enemy about the camp under cover of the darkness.

Bud was not, by nature, a blood-thirsty boy. All of these preparations for battle were made without the slightest thought of the actual effect of one of his missiles should it hit his mark. His industry was inspired more by the mechanical act than by any picture of human pain that might result. Hence, when the time came for him to make use of his weapon "with deadly intent," he found himself in a hesitant frame of mind. He knew that some animal, human or otherwise, was eyeing the camp with studied interest, and it was difficult to imagine other than a human being capable of such interest.

Bud finally came to the conclusion that the animal half hidden in the shadow of the bushes was a man, and that the latter's interest was centered in "Captain" Howard, whom he doubtless believed to be held prisoner within the four canvas walls of the tent.

"I bet he's one of those four men that took Hal and me and marooned us on that other island," the boy mused. "Of course, he's looking for a chance to set our prisoner free, but he's doomed to disappointment. My goodness!"

Bud whirled around suddenly as a new possibility occurred to him, stimulated by a slight noise like the cautious tread of a man's foot. The next instant a cry of alarm almost escaped him as he saw a human form near the entrance of the tent.

"My goodness!" he repeated aloud, but in subdued tone, as he recognized the approaching youth. "You'd better announce yourself, Max, before you come onto an armed person under such circumstances as these."

"Armed!" echoed the Canadian youth in surprise. "I thought Mr.

Perry said—"

"Oh, yes, he said we couldn't have his automatic, but I've been busy making a very effective substitute since I came out here—see?"

Bud exhibited his weapon by drawing back the leather sling, thereby stretching the elastics to their full capacity. His searchlight he had switched off after finishing the work on his catapult, and the only illumination in the open area came from the moon over the tree tops.

"Did you make that out here to-night?" demanded Max in astonishment.

"Sure—why not?" was the other's reply.

"Well, you're some boy, all right. I'd never 'ave thought of it. If anybody means mischief around here, he'd better look out, with a weapon like that in your hands."

"You bet he had," Bud returned with a sturdiness of purpose, indicating to his Canadian friend that he meant business. "And there's at least one prawler around here already. I'm glad you came out here, for I was just about to come in and wake up the whole camp."

"Is that so?" whispered Max. "Why, what's doing?"

"I don't want to let on that I know anybody is prowling about," Bud replied; "but if you'll watch those bushes straight south of here for a while you'll make out the form of a man half hidden there. He moves a little every now and then. Be careful and don't let him know you known he's there."

"I won't," Max replied excitedly. "Why don't you shoot at him?"

"I don't want to do that unless I have to," Bud replied. "Besides, I'd like to know what he's up to. Why did you come out here? Couldn't you sleep?"

"I didn't sleep a wink; I couldn't. My head was in a whirl all the time. I was busy imagining just such things as this. Believe me, it was some spooky job, out here all alone."

"Yes, that's true," Bud agreed. "I'm glad enough to have your company. By the way, you haven't explained how you happened to come here with Mr. Perry. We're mighty glad to have you here, but I was wondering how your folks happened to let you come."

"Mr. Buckley is my uncle," Max replied. "I called him up and told him what was going on out here, and he asked me to come along."

"Oh, that's it," Bud returned. "I was wondering if you Canadian boys are way ahead of us Yankee boys when it comes to doing as you please. My father wouldn't let me come on this trip if Mr. Perry hadn't come along."

"I guess we're not much different from you Yankees," Max replied. "But, talkin' about doing as you please, it seems to me that you went pretty far when you made that slingshot after Mr. Perry said you mustn't have a pistol."

"Oh, that's nothing like a pistol," Bud replied. "You couldn't kill anybody with it."

"I don't know about that," Max answered with a shake of his head. "I wouldn't like to be in front of it when you shot. I bet you could knock a fellow silly with it."

"Maybe I could. Well, anyway, a slingshot's a long way from being a pistol. Have you made that fellow out yet?"

"Yes, you bet I have," answered Max. "I've seen 'im move several times."

"Let's sit down and pretend not to suspect that anybody's watching us,"

Bud proposed. "Then maybe he'll be a little bolder."

"All right, but we'll have to keep a close watch out of the corner of our eyes."

"Sure. Come on. Here are a couple of chairs."

"Let's sit down facing each other, so that nobody can creep onto us unawares," suggested Max.

"That's a good idea," said Bud.

They seated themselves, face to face and within "whispering distance" of each other and continued their conversation in low tones, but at the same time keeping a sharp lookout for developments.

"This experience has proved one thing," Bud remarked in the course of their continued discussion, "and that is that all our watches ought to be in two's."

"Yes, a single watcher gets pretty lonesome, and, besides, it's too easy for him to be taken by surprise. Now, there's a sample of what I say. Don't look yet; he'll know we see him. He's moved, farther to the east, and now he's creeping up behind the tent."

"We must make sure that he's alone, or else rouse the rest of the camp," said Bud excitedly. "Keep watch in every direction. I'll turn slowly and get a look at him, and then turn back and pretend not to see him."

This program was observed carefully for a minute or two. Meanwhile the spy crept closer and closer, crawling like a serpentine quadruped and making fairly good progress withal. At last, however, Bud decided that it was time for him to do something to put a stop to this proceeding.

Without giving his companion any warning as to his intention, he lifted the catapult eye-line high, pulled back the sling, in which all this time he had held a stone nearly half the size of a hen's egg, and let it fly.

Thud!

That the missile hit the mark hard was indicated, first, by the sound of the blow, itself, and, second, by the muffled cry of agony that followed. The next instant the victim, who seemed to be struggling to retain his "quadruped balance," rolled over with a moan of impotent agony.

CHAPTER XXVI

The Sling Shot Victim

"What's the matter, boys?"

Mr. Perry appeared at the entrance of the tent with this question on his lips. The boys turned quickly, while Cub's father advanced nearer to pursue his inquiry.

"I shot somebody," Bud replied.

"Shot somebody!" Mr. Perry exclaimed. "What with?"

"This," the boy answered, exhibiting his slingshot. "Some fellow was prowling around here and I thought it was time to stop him. He was standing in those bushes over there for a long time, and I suppose he thought he was fully concealed, but I saw him. Then he started to crawl up close to the tent, and I let him have a good solid, heavy stone. It went like a bullet—these rubbers are awful strong, and I pulled them way back."

"He isn't killed; he's crawling away," Max interrupted at this point.

"We mustn't allow that," declared Bud. "We must find out who he is and what he was up to."

Just then Hal and Cub appeared on the scene, and a few words sufficed to explain to them what had occurred. All of the campers on retiring had kept on their day clothes, in order that they might be ready for action in case of trouble in the night.

"Come on, we must stop him," Cub announced.

This seemed to be the opinion of all, including Mr. Perry, and a general move was made in the direction of the slowly retreating injured spy. They soon overtook him and threw a flood of illumination about him with their search-lights, which they had picked up in the dark almost as instinctively as a grandmother picks up her glasses in the morning.

"Why, he's a boy!"

Bud was the only one present who gave utterance to this discovery aloud, but the "exclamation" flashed mentally in the head of every other youthful investigator in the group. As Mr. Perry was not easily mystified, we must take it for granted that he was not easily astonished, so that probably he did not feel like giving vent to anything of the nature of an exclamation.

"Well," said the latter quietly; "we must take this youngster back to the camp and give him some hospital treatment. Can you walk?" he added, addressing the victim of Bud's slingshot.

"You don't think I'd be down here if I could, do you?" moaned the fellow sarcastically. "But just wait till I get over this and I'll fix the fellow that hit me."

"Let's not waste any time with him here," urged Mr. Perry. "Some of you boys pick him up carefully, so as not to hurt him, and carry him into the tent. We'll give him a quizzing there."

All the young members of the Catwhisker party had had first aid instruction, so that they knew how to lift the injured boy and carry him with a minimum of pain to the sufferer. A minute later the victim was lying on one of the cots in the tent, with his captors gathered around him, undoubtedly more concerned about the mystery of his presence than in the extent of his injuries.

"No, boys, we mustn't try to get his story from him until we take care of his wound and see to it that he is resting easy"; Mr. Perry interposed.

Accordingly the wound was examined and found to consist of a very bad bruise on the side of the right hip. Bud's missile had struck the intruder at a point where there was little flesh, right on a protruding ridge of the hip bone, and it was easy to see that the blow must have been very painful.

"I don't think it's very serious," Mr. Perry remarked after examining the wound; "but I doubt if this boy will want to be running around very much for several days. About all we can do is to apply some liniment to the wound and encourage it, by careful treatment, to heal as rapidly as possible."

A bottle of liniment was accordingly produced and an application administered by Mr. Perry. This seemed to ease the prisoner-patient somewhat, although he made no effort to stand up, or even to sit up.

"He may have a bone fracture," Mr. Perry remarked, after he had finished his first-aid ministration, "It's a pretty bad wound, after all. We'll have to take him to the nearest physician in the morning if he doesn't show decided improvement by that time. I didn't dare rub the liniment in because the slightest touch was so painful."

"The skin isn't broken," Bud observed, with a tone of real concern, for, in spite of the fact that the fellow was there on no friendly mission, the catapult "dead shot" now felt no exultation over his deed.

"No, or I could not have used the liniment," Mr. Perry replied. "His clothing protected him against a broken wound. By the way," he continued, turning to the victim, who lay on one of the camp cots that formed a part of the regular equipment of the Catwhisker; "who are you and what were you doing here?"

"Never you mind who I am or what I was doing here," snapped the youth, who appeared to be a few years older than the boy Catwhiskerites and their Canadian friend, Max. "You wait till my father gets after you. He'll clean you all up."

"And who may your father be?" inquired Mr. Perry with provoking calmness.

"You'll find out who my father is, just you wait. You haven't any right here. These islands belong to my father and—"

"Oh—ho!" interrupted Mr. Perry in tone of sudden discovery. "So that's the way the wind blows, is it? I get you now. You're the son of one of those kidnappers."

The boy's face twitched, possibly with pain, more likely with alarm at his having betrayed his identity so foolishly.

"We'll get down to the bottom of this mystery yet," Cub declared confidently.

"Yes, all we need is a little mathematics, Mr. Perry, and we'll soon solve the problem."

"We've had some mathematics already," Mr. Perry smiled.

"I didn't see it," returned Cub. "Maybe I'm slow."

"No, you haven't got farther than your One's in the addition table. You can add 1 to any other number, but you can't tell how much 2 plus 2 are."

"All right, I'm foolish," admitted Cub. "Spring your joke."

"This is a rather serious situation in which to spring a joke," reminded the "foolish boy's" father. "But didn't you hear me put two and two together when this fellow declared that this island belonged to his father?"

Laughter greeted this sally, in spite of the seriousness of the situation.

"By the way, I wonder if we haven't got this youngster's father a prisoner on the Catwhisker," Mr. Perry continued. Then he turned toward the youth on the cot and inquired:

"Is your father a tall, angular fellow with a smart, flip way of talking, and do his friends call him captain?"

The catapult victim did not answer, but the expression on his face was all the evidence that was needed to indicate what an honest reply would have been.

"I thought so," said Mr. Perry. "Now, would you like to make a trip down to the landing and occupy a stateroom in the Catwhisker with your father? The Catwhisker, by the way, is a yacht in which we made a trip from Oswego, New York, to rescue a boy marooned by some young scamps on this island. After he was marooned, your father and his friends kidnapped him and took him away. Now, what we want to know is, where is he?"

Still the wounded prisoner made no reply.

"There's going to be some awful serious trouble for your outfit if that boy isn't returned," Mr. Perry went on, waxing fiercer and more fierce in his manner as he purposely worked up a towering rage for the sake of its effect on the boy on the cot. "Would you like me to turn you over to the father of the boy whom your scoundrel gang kidnapped? What do you think would happen to you if he got hold of you? Well, he's on the boat down at the landing, and your father is there too, under lock and key. And before long we're going to have the whole gang of you under lock and key. Now, don't you think it is best for you to give up your secret and tell where that boy is?"

The prisoner was now thoroughly frightened. He shrunk away from the glowering owner of the Catwhisker as if he feared the man's clenched fists were about to rain blows on his wounded body. At last he gasped in trembling tones:

"I don't know, I don't know."

"Don't know what?" thundered Mr. Perry.

"I don't know—I don't know—where he is," stuttered the terrified boy.

"And I don't believe you, young sir. Do you understand me? You're not telling the truth. Come on, boys, we'll turn him over to the father of the boy they kidnapped."

"Oh, no, no; don't, please don't, mister," pleaded the scared youngster. "I don't know where that boy is; please sir, I don't. But I'll ask my father to tell if you'll take me to him."

"There, I thought we'd get something out of you," said Mr. Perry in tone of satisfaction.

"But you didn't do it with mathematics this time, dad," Cub declared in a voice that indicated full confidence of victory.

"Oh, yes, I did, my youthful minus quality," his father flashed back. "I multiplied my wrath very righteously, and this fellow is going to have his woes multiplied and his joys subtracted and his peace of mind divided into a thousand more pieces if he doesn't get busy on the square and see to it that young Alvin Baker is returned to his father."

"He isn't hurt nearly as bad as he pretends to be, Mr. Perry," Hal put in as the "mathematical man" indicated that he had "spoken his speech". "He moved his leg several times. You better watch out or he'll be jumping up and making a dash for liberty."

"I'd been noticing that," Mr. Perry replied. "I wouldn't insult Bud's catapulting powers by intimating that this fellow wasn't pretty badly hurt; but I do think we've overestimated the extent of the injury. He was completely knocked out by the blow, but he's been recovering here pretty rapidly. Come on, now, Master Howard—what's your first name—won't tell, eh?—all right; we'll find out in due time—come on, let's talk a walk down to papa and that terrible man whose claws are just aching for revenge for the loss of his son. What—you can't get up? Well, boys, pick him up again and carry him. Be careful, of course, for he's in some pain yet. Now, we'll march. Bud, you bring up the rear with your mediaeval rubber pistol, and I'll march beside you. If anybody, tries to interfere with us there'll be some crack-shot shooting."

Hal, Cub, Bud, and Max picked up the wounded boy in approved relief-ambulance-corps style and carried him, with a few groans and moans from their burden, across the open area, through the narrow belt of bushes, to the top of the hill that overlooked the landing. There Mr. Perry called a halt and then hailed the yacht thus:

"Ahoy, the Catwhisker."

All listened breathlessly, but no answer came. Then the owner of the boat put greater volume in his voice and repeated the hail:

"Ahoy, the Catwhisker! Ahoy, the Catwhisker!"

This time an answer came, but hardly in the manner expected.

A muffled, rattling, rackety noise came from within the cabin, the door of which seemed to be closed. It sounded as if someone were pounding and kicking the walls like an insane patient in an unpadded room.

"What in the world does that mean?" Cub demanded, giving utterance to the apprehension that thrilled every other member of the party.

"I don't know," his father replied; "but I'm going to find out pretty quick. You boys stay here with the prisoner. I'm going down there to investigate."

With this announcement, he drew his automatic for ready use and began to descend the steps they had fashioned in the stony hill before establishing their camp on Friday Island.

CHAPTER XXVII

Chased Out

The investigation did not take long. The boys watched Mr. Perry as he crossed the moonlit deck of the Catwhisker and entered the cabin. A few minutes later he returned on the deck and with him were two men, whom the observers on shore recognized as Mr. Baker and the Canadian officer. Then Mr. Perry called out:

"Come on down here, boys."

A minute later they were on board the yacht with their prisoner. Cub, the most impatient of their number, was first to speak.

"What's the matter?" he asked.

"Matter enough," growled the officer. "Those scoundrels outwitted us, locked us in the stateroom, and our prisoner is gone."

The boys were so astonished that not one of them uttered a sound.

"I haven't heard their story yet," Mr. Perry interposed. "We'll all get it together."

"It won't take long to tell how they did it," Mr. Buckley began. Then he seemed to hesitate, glancing in some embarrassment at Mr. Baker.

"I'll take all the blame," the latter confessed at this juncture. "In fact, there's nobody to blame but me. I wasn't asleep at my post, but my wits must have been slumbering, for one of those fellows stole up behind me and gave me a rap on the head that put me to sleep sure enough. When I woke up I was in a pitch dark stateroom, with the door locked. Luckily my searchlight had not been taken out of my pocket, and soon I had the place well enough lighted to determine where I was. I also found something else; I found Mr. Buckley in the same condition that I had been in—unconscious. Mr. Buckley can tell you the rest."

"There's absolutely nothing for me to tell," Mr. Buckley replied, "I went to sleep on the cot in the cabin and woke up with a headache in the stateroom. Mr. Baker was working over me as if I'd been shell-shocked on the battlefield. I think we both were sandbagged, for there were no bruises on our heads. We were locked in and probably would have been driven to the necessity of breaking the door open if Mr. Perry hadn't come when he did and let us out."

"I found both the stateroom door and the cabin door locked with the keys on the outside," Mr. Perry explained. "Well, we have this consolation at least: While we were losing one prisoner, we were capturing another."

"What do you mean by that?" Mr. Buckley; demanded quickly.

"Here's the new prisoner right here," was the other's reply, indicating the catapult victim who had suddenly found himself able to stand with his weight on his uninjured leg and aided by two of the Catwhisker boys.

"Who is he—one of that gang?" asked the officer.

"He's a son of one of them, probably the one who was rescued from you."

"Lock him up in that stateroom at once, and I'll have something more to tell you," Mr. Buckley ordered.

The order was speedily obeyed; then all gathered eagerly about the government officer.

"The situation is this," the latter began. "When those rascals raided this boat they robbed me of my gun and I suppose they got yours, too, didn't they, Mr. Baker?"

The father of the missing freshman slapped his hand on his "pistol pocket" and then gasped:

"Yes, it's gone."

"I thought so," continued the officer. "Now, we have an armed enemy to contend with. If they get wind of the fact that we have the son of one of them a prisoner on this yacht, you can expect a fusillade of bullets popping through your portholes any time. My advice is to get out of here as soon as possible."

"Where'll we go?" asked Mr. Perry.

"We'll decide that after we get away. If you want to keep your prisoner, don't stay here."

"Dad's got his automatic yet," Cub reminded with youthful confidence in a chamber full of shells.

"And I've got my slingshot," chimed in Bud.

"Tee-hee," laughed Hal.

"Oh you can laugh all you want to, Tee-hee, but if it hadn't been for my slingshot, we wouldn't have any prisoner at all right now," Bud flung back with a suggestion of resentment.

"Yes, we must give Bud credit for all he's done," Mr. Perry agreed. "We owe a good deal to his ingenuity."

"We ought to take our prisoner over to Rockport and put him in jail," suggested Mr. Baker.

"On what ground?" asked Mr. Buckley. "What would you charge him with? He hasn't done anything except spy around your camp here. You couldn't put him in jail for that and keep him there any time. Besides, his father claims to own these islands—maybe he does."

"Well, what are you in favor of doing?" asked Mr. Baker.

"I think we ought to move your entire camp outfit to this boat and then stand off from the shore for a while and keep our eyes on this place with spyglasses—have you got a pair?"

"Yes," Mr. Perry replied; "two good strong pair."

"Then we'd better get busy at once before they suspect what has become of this boy we have here."

"All right, let's get busy at once," said Mr. Perry. "The boys, however, must stay here on the boat. We don't want to run any risk of their falling into the hands of the enemy."

"Oh, Mr. Perry, let me go along with you and get my radio outfit,"

Hal begged.

The yachtsman looked at the pleading youth for a few moments in hesitating manner.

"I don't know," he replied slowly. "Still, I suppose we could protect one of you if anything happened. Well, inasmuch as we men don't know anything about disconnecting a radio hook-up. I guess we'll take you for one trip. Come on; no more delay. Keep a good lookout, Cub and Bud, and set up a holler if anything goes wrong. And, Bud, be careful not to mistake us for the enemy when we return; we don't want to be hit by that sling of yours."

"We ought to have a signal, so we could be sure to recognize each other,"

Bud suggested.

"All right, what'll it be?"

"The Catwhisker ought to have an official signal," said Hal. "Why not make it 'meow'?"

"Very good; it's adopted."

The first trip was made without incident worthy of special note. Hal and Mr. Baker brought all of the radio set except the aerial, and Mr. Perry and Mr. Buckley each carried a load of camp equipment on their return trip. Then Mr. Perry insisted that Hal remain on the yacht, and the three men went ashore again for another load.

But from this trip they came back sooner than looked for, and the manner of their return alarmed the boys, who expected momentarily to hear pistol shots fired at them from the shore. The three men came down the hill to the landing almost at a run, and as they reached the deck, Mr. Perry announced in cautious tones:

"Boys, we'll have to leave that camp as it is for a while. Those men are up there watching for us. We don't want to get into a gun battle with them; so we're going to back out of here as fast as we can."

CHAPTER XXVIII

A Radio Eavesdropper

The Catwhisker was backed out of the narrow inlet or strait, in which she had been moored, without interference on the part of the hostile men on Friday Island. Whether or not the latter knew of the departure of the yacht, the men and boys on board had no way to determine. It is probable, however, that they heard the coughing and sputtering of the gasoline engine and that they watched proceedings from any of the numerous places of concealment afforded by rocks, bushes, and trees along the shore elevations.

At any rate, the most careful scrutiny of the deep shadows revealed nothing to the Catwhiskerites and their guests as the yacht worked its way out of the inclosure, and presently they exchanged congratulations one with another on the assurance that they were well out of pistol-shot range from the group of islands.

"How far do you think we had better go?" asked Mr. Perry addressing the Canadian officer after this matter of concern had been well taken care of.

"Oh, I think we ought to find a mooring place at some island about a mile from here and try to get a little sleep before daybreak," Mr. Buckley replied. "I'm sure Mr. Baker and I need some brain rest after the slams we got on our craniums. I've got the worst headache right now that I ever had in my life."

"So have I," Mr. Baker chimed in.

"All right, let's not discuss this affair any more to-night," Mr. Perry proposed. "Boys, you may as well get your wits together to arrange the most comfortable sleeping quarters possible under the circumstances. I guess about all our bedding is at the camp."

The boys set about to do as suggested, but it was not long before they realized that wits could do little for them regarding rest convenience for the remainder of the night. Presently they reported back the following results to Mr. Perry:

One lounge in the cabin, bedding enough for one of the berths and enough other bedding and articles of clothing to be rolled into pillow substitutes for half a dozen sleepers.

Presently Mr. Buckley, who had been keeping a sharp lookout ahead in the moonlight, supplemented by the strong headlight of the Catwhisker, pointed out what seemed to be a suitable mooring place for the yacht for the rest of the night, and a careful run-in was made, accompanied by pole-soundings to prevent running aground. The depth proved to be O.K., and in a short time the yacht was tied up to a small tree which leaned over almost far enough to dip some of its branches into the water. As all were eager to waste no time belonging to nature's nocturnal period of rest, the pillow substitutes were soon rolled and the various sleeping quarters assigned according to varying degrees of necessity. Because of their "sand-bag headaches," Mr. Baker and Mr. Buckley were given the cabin lounge and the available stateroom berth. Although they felt reasonably safe against further intrusion in their new quarters, nevertheless it was deemed wise to maintain a series of one-hour watches, the first of which fell to Mr. Perry by his own choice. Before the general retirement of all but the first watch, an inspection was made of the stateroom prison, and the boy prisoner was found to be fast asleep on the floor with one arm for a pillow.

Hal was given the last watch, beginning shortly before the break of day. Bud who had preceded him, handed over his slingshot together with a supply of stones which he had brought in one of his pockets from Friday Island. Hal accepted the catapult with profound respect, expressing full confidence in his ability to repel a formidable array of would-be boarders with a weapon of such knock-out record.

After it was light enough for him to see what he was doing, Hal occupied his time by connecting his radio set for service on the yacht once more. When this task was completed, he set about to prepare breakfast, deciding that he would let the sleepers get another hour's rest, as he could prepare the morning meal alone almost as quickly as with the aid of one or two others. He had already learned the truth of the housewife's axiom that "two are a crowd in a kitchen, and three are a throng."

At 7 o'clock he called all the sleepers to breakfast. The two "sand-bag headaches" were no more, and everybody was as cheerful as could have been expected under the circumstances.

"What are we going to do about Bud's prisoner?" Hal inquired as they were about to gather around the cabin table, which was well loaded with appetizing dishes, some of them steaming hot.

"Oh, we'll have to give him some breakfast," replied Mr. Perry, starting for the prison-stateroom. "I'd quite forgotten him."

Without more ado, the prisoner was produced and supplied with conveniences to prepare for the morning meal. After he had washed and combed his tousled hair, he presented a fairly respectable appearance and was given a place at the table. He sat through the meal without as much as a "thank you" for dishes passed to him, and the other breakfasters, observing that he was in anything but a cheerful mood, did not attempt to draw him into conversation.

After breakfast the three men on board held a conference, the result of which was an agreement to run back to the Friday Island group and make an inspection of it with glasses from every possible angle. In this way they hoped to be able to obtain a clew relative to the headquarters and activities of the men who had ordered them to move their camp from Friday Island. Then the engine was started, and the course of the Catwhisker directed up stream.

"Now, my friend," remarked Mr. Buckley, addressing the young Canadian; "you'd be perfectly welcome to the freedom of the deck under ordinary circumstances, but the present are extraordinary circumstances, so we'll have to ask you to resort to the pleasures and comforts of the cabin. Boys," he added, addressing the three young Catwhiskerites, "you may go into the cabin, too, and get acquainted with him." Then in lower tone to Cub, who stood near the officer, he suggested: "Maybe he'll be more talkative with you boys than he has been with us men. See if you can't get something out of him."

Cub "tipped" Hal and Bud as to the purpose communicated to him by the Canadian officer, and the three conducted "Bud's prisoner" into the cabin.

But the latter proved to be about as uncommunicative as he had been when the older members of the yacht's company tried to get something out of him. He appeared to be bright enough and not especially coarse grained, so that from the standpoint of quality qualifications, there seemed to be no reason for his sullenness. Hal frankly made a statement to him to this effect, but it produced no result of the kind desired and intended. They got only short, surly returns in response to their most friendly advances.

At last they gave it up and returned on deck. Before leaving the cabin, however, Cub said to the prisoner:

"Now, if you'll promise to stay here and not make any attempt to escape, we won't lock you up. Otherwise we'll have to lock you up in a stateroom."

"I'll promise," was the fellow's laconic response.

"By the way," Bud remarked, as they were about to leave the cabin, "would you mind telling us the handle of your name? We know your father's surname, but we'd like to know how to address you. You're too young for us to call you Mr. Howard."

"You c'n call me Bill, if you want to," the slingshot victim replied.

Hal was particularly impressed with a sly, cunning look in the eyes of the prisoner and told himself that the fellow would bear watching to keep him out of mischief.

"I tell you what I'd like to do," he said to his two friends as they reached the deck. "I'd like to hide in the closet in the cabin and watch that fellow. I bet he'd do something that would help us break his mysterious silence."

"You could steal down into that little alcove near the entrance of the cabin and watch him there through the crack in the door," Bud suggested.

"That's second best choice," said Hal, "I think I'll make use of it at once."

Accordingly he descended the companionway with the greatest caution and succeeded in ensconcing himself in the position suggested by Bud. He had not been there long when he was amply rewarded for his diligence.

He could hear the prisoner moving about in the cabin and a peep through the long narrow aperture along the hinge side of the door acquainted him with the object of the Canadian boy's interest. The latter, apparently, had just seated himself at the table, and with phones to his ears, was in the act of tuning the instrument.

Presently he appeared to be satisfied with this preliminary and put his hand on the sending key. The fellow seemed to be perfectly at home with the outfit. Now the key was tapping and the spark was leaping across the gap. The secret watcher leaned forward eagerly to catch every sound. Yes, it came in genuine enough dots and dashes, and he read them with ever increasing astonishment.

First the operator repeated a Canadian call several times. Then, apparently, the call was acknowledged, and he sent the following message:

"I am prisoner on yacht, Catwhisker, in hands of the fellows I tried to hold back, with radio, as they were leaving Oswego, N.Y. They are determined to solve mystery of your doings. Don't bother about me, but tell pa to clean out his place as soon as possible and then let his prisoner go. They have government officer with them on his trail and will soon find his hiding place and raid it."

"My goodness!" Hal breathed excitedly. "Now I'm getting at the bottom of this affair. That boy is the anonymous amateur who pretended to have a radio wager with Hal's cousin and tried to make us think his SOS was a joke."

CHAPTER XXIX

The End of the "Mystery"

Hal almost held his breath in his eagerness to maintain perfect silence in order that he might "listen-in" to this radio transmission until the sender had telegraphed all that he had in mind to send.

"My, if I only had an extension receiver," he thought. "How I would like to hear what the fellow he's talking with has to say."

Even as this longing came to his mind, "Bill" ceased to send and listened attentively to something that was coming to him "over the wireless." Presently he swung the aerial switch over and began to send again.

"I tell you you are in danger," he dot-and-dashed. "That hiding place is not safe any more. They will have a revenue cutter down on you, before you know what has happened. The government officer suspects the truth, I am dead sure."

A few more sentences of similar purport were sent in reply to other messages received. Then "Bill" cut the radio conversation short with a warning that he did not dare continue it longer and left the table. As he got up from his seat, Hal stepped into the cabin and remarked:

"Congratulations, 'Bill'; I didn't know you were a radio fan. But really,

I'm glad to recognize you as an old acquaintance."

"Bill" turned as white as the proverbial sheet and trembled like the aspen of similar associations. Then he blurted out:

"I don't know what you mean."

"Do you deny that you were just telegraphing a message to a friend of yours?" Hal demanded.

"No, not at all," replied "Bill". "I guess that ought to convince you I'm not the criminal you're trying to make me out to be."

"I'm not trying to make you out a criminal. I surely hope you're not. No, I don't believe there are many criminals among radio fans and college students."

"College students!"

"Say, 'Bill Howard', don't try to play the innocent to a fellow who's been listening-in to your unconscious confessions ever since you began to talk in your sleep," Hal scoffed with well simulated disgust. "I know well enough who you are. You're one of the sophomores of Edward's College who hazed Alvin Baker by marooning him on that island where his cousin shot you with a slingshot."

"Bill's" lower jaw dropped, and there was some more aspen trembling in his frame.

"You don't need to be so badly scared," Hal went on with a tone of reassurance inspired by a purpose. "Of course that was a pretty raw hazing, but you can get by with it yet if you don't carry your prank any farther. Tell us where your victim is."

"Give me a few days and I'll produce him," the frightened boy pleaded.

"He isn't hurt, and nobody's goin' to hurt 'im."

"Well, I'm glad to get that much out of you," Hal declared with profound gratification. "But I don't see why in the world you have to be so mysterious about it. Why not tell me now where he is?"

"I—I—can't," faltered the other.

"Don't you know?"

"No, but I can find out."

Hal was sure the fellow was lying, and he looked at him with accusing penetration.

"You'll have to let me do it my own way," the Canadian youth added stubbornly.

Realizing that he could make no further progress with the prisoner at present, and fearing that it might not be wise to disclose what more he had learned by listening to the wireless messages the hazer had just sent, Hal returned to the deck and recounted his experience in the cabin to his companions. All were assembled at the pilot house when he gave his recital.

"This is important," said Mr. Buckley when the account was finished. "I'm glad you didn't disclose to him the fact that you suspect anything is going on of interest to the Canadian government. He won't be on his guard so much perhaps as he would be if you had put all your cards on the table. By the way, everything seems to be happening in our favor right now. There's a Canadian revenue boat over there. Let's run over that way and hail it."

The boat in question was somewhat larger than the Catwhisker and looked as if it might give the yacht a merry race if the two were matched for a test of speed. She was 300 yards distant and in a few minutes the evicted Friday Islanders had run up within short hailing distance of her. Then Buckley gave a signal, which was recognized, and the two boats were brought close together. A short conversation between Buckley and the commander of the revenue boat was sufficient to acquaint the latter with the situation, and he promised to remain in the vicinity in order that he might come speedily to the aid of the Catwhisker when needed.

Then began the work of careful examination of the Friday Island group with binoculars. The yacht was only a few hundred yards from these islands when the Canadian revenue cutter was sighted. After arrangements for co-operation had been made with the commander of this boat, the Catwhisker began to move slowly around the group, while Mr. Perry and Mr. Buckley examined every detail of their littoral features with strong glasses. Cub was at the wheel, and Mr. Baker, Bud, Hal and Max stood near the two men with the glasses, eagerly waiting for significant results.

"I wonder if this is to be the finishing stroke," said Bud, addressing the two boys near him.

Mr. Perry overheard the "wonder" and replied:

"I am confident that we will solve the whole problem very shortly."

"With mathematics?" asked Hal.

"You see we are moving in a geometric circle, do you not?" Mr. Perry returned with a smile.

"Oh, look there!" suddenly exclaimed Max. "A motor boat."

But there was no need of calling attention to so conspicuous an appearance. All saw it at the same time. It darted out from a narrow passage between two of the smaller islands surrounding the one that Alvin Baker had denominated "Friday." It was a small cabin runabout, very neatly designed and constructed; and apparently with a draft measured only by inches. She made directly for the yacht.

"Catwhisker, ahoy!" called out a youthful voice, and a wide-awake red-haired boy put his head out of one of the port windows of the cabin. "I want to come aboard with important information."

Of course, everybody aboard the Catwhisker was astonished, but Mr. Perry signaled Cub to reverse the engine. This was done, and the yacht soon lost all headway. Then the runabout glided close up to the larger power boat, and the boy who had hailed her sprang over the two adjacent rails. Another boy could be seen in the pilot seat of the smaller craft.

"My name is Halstone," announced the visitor. "I am from—"

His announcement was drowned with exclamations of surprise from his audience.

"Hal Stone!" repeated several in chorus, including the Catwhisker's Hal

Stone himself.

"Yes, Halstone," reiterated the challenged youth; Frederick Halstone. "Anything funny about that? I'm the reporter from Watertown who was dot-and-dashing with you folks last night. I got in touch with a friend of mine right away who owns that motor boat, and he was crazy to make the trip here after this big scoop. I'm here representing not only my paper, but the Associated Press. We located Friday Island here without any difficulty. But I brought my radio outfit and loop antenna along and listened in just a short time ago to some messages between somebody who said he was a prisoner on the Catwhisker and another fellow on a boat in the cove I just came out of. You'd hardly think a boat of its size could get in there. It's about the same size as the Catwhisker, and is built and painted like it. I think you'll find the solution of your big mystery is right there. They're loading a lot of stuff in boxes from a cave in the steep bank of that small island next to the big one. The cove is between these two small islands, which, you see, have high banks and are covered with bushes and trees, so that their boat could rest there and be invisible to anybody out on the river or on the shore of the larger island that you call 'Friday'. They're making a big hustle to get away."

"Is there a boy in there?" asked Mr. Baker eagerly.

"Yes, several of them and four men. The men were pretty sore at me for running in there, and they ordered me out. I don't think, however, that there's much love lost between the men and the boys. I suspect the men are smugglers, and the boys have got into a scrape they don't like. There was an exchange of hot words going on just as I ran into their hiding place."

No more time was wasted in the making of explanations. The little revenue cutter was signaled and in less than fifteen minutes half a dozen men, including Mr. Buckley and Mr. Baker, were on the cabin-runabout which again saucily invaded the retreat of the Catwhisker's "double."

CHAPTER XXX

The Result of a Radio Hazing

The raid was a speedy success. "Captain" Howard and his crew of lawbreakers offered no resistance when they saw the odds against them, for each of the men from the revenue cutter was armed and promised to shoot to kill if a hostile hand was raised against them.

Then they made an inspection of the cave, which was of considerable size and lighted with an oil lamp, and there the lost victim of a radio college hazing was found chained to a post that had been driven into the ground floor. He had not suffered from malicious mistreatment in any way, but was chafing under restraint and confinement. He was a little older than the Catwhisker boys, but he had no "college airs" and was soon telling his story as one boy to a group of chums, while the men stood around and drank it all in as eagerly as if they themselves were boys again.

"Bill Howard made the biggest mistake of his life when he confederated with three other sophomores to haze me," Alvin began. "He didn't know his father had a hide-out here when they marooned me on Friday Island. His father owns several motor boats that are used for pleasure excursions, but, I suspect, he wasn't making money fast enough and fell for a scheme put up to him from the other men who are now his companions in crime. They were in touch with a gang of burglars and hold-up men who wanted a means of disposing of their loot. They induced Mr. Howard to consent to the use of one of his boats to convey stolen property of various kinds to this cave as a hiding place, and from here, occasionally, to places of disposal, principally in the United States. Well, Bill's band of hazers unwittingly brought me to these islands, and before long there was a pretty mix-up. The operators of this burglars' 'fence' found me on Friday Island and got the idea, I suppose, that I was spying on them. At first I hoped they would let me go, but I made some foolish remarks, based merely on suspicion, about the character of their business, and they concluded the jig was up and brought me right to this cave, and, of course, after that I could see everything that was going on. Then the hazers appeared on the scene. I suppose they became a little nervous about me. I gathered from conversation I overheard that they stumbled into this place while searching for me and then they were taken partly into the confidence of the lawbreakers. But they're pretty smart boys, if they are sophomores and if their leader is a son of a smuggler of stolen goods, and soon were putting two and two together—"

"More mathematics," interrupted Mr. Perry gravely.

Alvin looked at him curiously, but this was no time for academic digression, and the veiled quip had to await later explanation.

Of course there was more discussion of the strange tangle of events, which now seemed to be about to be cleared up. Indeed, it took many days for them to thrash the subject out completely, but it would hardly do to write another book on matters now essentially explained so we must leave those details to the diversion of Friday Island camp.

The camp was rehabitated, Hal's radio outfit was hooked up again with the island aerial, and all of the Catwhiskerites and their newly discovered radio friends enjoyed a week's undisturbed outing in the midst of recent personal romantic associations.

As for the "radio hazers," they went back home with no spirit of "brag" over their achievements, and the members of the band of smugglers of stolen goods were held in custody and eventually punished under sentences returned in a Canadian court.

Meanwhile Mr. Perry took steps looking toward the purchase of the Friday Island group from the Canadian government as a summer camping place for the Catwhiskerites and their friends.

Milton Keynes UK
Ingram Content Group UK Ltd.
UKHW020837260624
444769UK00011B/345